CRANNÓG 46 au~~··~~ 9017

GW00367982

Editorial

Sandra Bu.
Ger Burke
Jarlath Fahy
Tony O'Dwyer

ISSN 1649-4865
ISBN 978-1-907017-48-3

Cover image: 'Resistance' by Jayashree Rai
Cover image sourced by Sandra Bunting
Cover design by Wordsonthestreet
Published by Wordsonthestreet for Crannóg magazine
www.wordsonthestreet.com @wordsstreet

Comhairle Cathrach na Gaillimhe
Galway City Council

CONTENTS

The Galway Study Centre

Since 1983, the Galway Study Centre has been dedicating itself to giving an excellent education service to post-primary school students in Galway.

info@galwaystudycentre.ie
Tel: 091-564254

www.galwaystudycentre.ie

Submissions for Crannóg 47 open November 1st until November 30th

Publication date is March 2nd 2018

Crannóg is published three times a year in spring, summer and autumn.

Submission Times: Month of November for spring issue. Month of March for summer issue. Month of July for autumn issue.

We will <u>not read</u> submissions sent outside these times.

POETRY: *Send no more than three poems. Each poem should be under 50 lines.*

PROSE: *Send one story. Stories should be under 2,000 words.*

We do not accept postal submissions.

When emailing your submission we require **three** *things:*

1. *The text of your submission included both in body of email and as a Word attachment (this is to ensure correct layout. We may, however, change your layout to suit our publication).*

2. *A brief bio in the third person. Include this both in body and in attachment.*

3. *A postal address for contributor's copy in the event of publication.*

To learn more about Crannóg Magazine, or purchase copies of the current issue, log on to our website:

www.crannogmagazine.com

THE MIDDLE-WHITE   STEVE WADE

If she were on the farm, she'd be a two-toed ungulate: a middle-white pig, as pink and soft looking as a marsh mellow, swollen and healthy and primed to drop a litter of piglets.

Three weeks now since he had completed the construction of the compound, Gideon Gilligan didn't like to spend too much time in any of the towns he had been exploring. Sometimes he just drove through without stopping. Otherwise, he parked his Pajero on the outskirts, and walked to its centre, his fixed gaze before him, seemingly unaware or disinterested in everything about him.

But his reason for being there was as purposeful as a marauding lion's moving across the Serengeti. Through his peripheral vision, he homed in on those with potential.

With an expert eye for healthy livestock, he measured their potential at a glance: Sturdy-boned, with rolls of flesh about their limbs, their haunches wide, good teeth, and a healthy shine to the eye were the qualities that he sought. There were a number of females who displayed these physical attributes, but they lacked one other particular necessity to complete Gilligan's ideal. Never a man to settle for less than his expectations, he held out until she presented herself.

Ready to quit the hunt and return home quarryless, the day she finally showed up, his focus had switched to other things. The autumn evening had turned chilly, and he was without his jacket. He felt the cold burrowing under his shirt at the neck. He couldn't afford to be sick. Not ever. Should anyone other than him be required to tend the livestock, all his plans would come undone.

'Fuck this shit anyway,' he said aloud, hawked up something bitter from his throat, and spat into the pavement. He glanced quickly about him. His lapse, luckily, had drawn no unwanted attention. That's when the thing that slept in a nest at the backs of his eyes awoke. He twisted his wrist to look at his watch. Almost five o'clock. The Angelus bells would be chiming before the evening news by the time he got home. Another afternoon wasted. The furry thing with sharp teeth began to gnaw at the tissue attached to his skull. The cows would already be gathered at the gate, lowing to be milked. Inside his head, the trapped rat chewed with greater desperation. The flesh shavings sliced off by sharp teeth slipped down his throat and into his stomach, where they turned sour and festered.

And then he saw her. Coming out from a Tesco Express store, a chubby girl with thick hair the colour of a fox's coat. About her shoulders a white jacket, which she held at the throat like a cape. Her other hand rested on her swollen stomach. Weeks only, maybe days, before she was due to give birth. But she wasn't alone. Walking beside her, a nondescript dowdy girl who looked like a million other girls. Gilligan feigned checking his mobile, put it on silent, and, with the phone pressed to his ear, crossed the road and followed the two women at a respectable distance. A light rain began to fall.

He spoke in a low voice to nobody at the end of the line, and was close enough to the women to catch some of their words. Their voices were high and excited, crowded with Friday evening, new babies, clothes and family life. Coming to a small white pub, the nondescript woman asked the chubby one if she was sure she wouldn't. The other said she really had to get going, and that she'd see her on Sunday. The two laughed meaninglessly, said their goodbyes and waved stupidly into each other's face.

Gilligan felt the trapped rat dashing about inside his skull, its tiny offensive claws scrabbling for freedom. He crossed back to the other side of the road where tall trees and a long stretch of hedging created sections of shade that interspersed the haloed light thrown by the street-lamps; the perfect cover into which he could meld. It gave him protection too from the rain, which, without warning, had become torrential.

Although this wasn't how he had planned it, his instinct told him that the time to strike was now. His original plan, to stake out his quarry and study it from a distance, become aware of its movements and its idiosyncrasies, he could forego. Sometimes even the most experienced and cautious of hunters recognised when something was presented to them as though an offering from some unseen force.

When the woman, her white jacket now held over her head, turned into an alcove between an unlit building and what might have been a fenced-in park, Gilligan crossed back over to her side of the road. He heard the sound of a car door cracking open and the clunk of it being shut. Twisting his head about, he used his ears as much as his eyes. Apart from a car approaching in the distance, nothing and nobody.

And then, from where the woman and her car were hidden in the alcove, he heard the firing of an engine. Onto the shiny pavement there spilled a pool of light. The light changed from red to the white of reverse lights.

From his trousers pocket, Gilligan took the penknife he used for cutting his pipe tobacco. With his thumbnail, he worked the blade free and held it by his side. The woman's car began to reverse slowly, but braked as the car on the road whooshed by at speed. Gilligan slashed the blade across his own forearm, and ran fast at the again reversing car, while closing the knife.

As he half-vaulted, half-jumped over the car's rear, he slapped his hand hard on the boot. Accustomed to tumbling safely on the ground from his rugby days, he pocketed the knife and rolled about on the pavement.

The woman was out of her car, her hands to the sides of her head, and asking in a high-pitched voice if he was okay. She didn't see him, she told him. And asked excitedly if he needed an ambulance.

'No,' Gilligan said. 'It's just my arm.' He took his palm away from where he had pressed it. The open wound now a black and soggy mess from his fall to the ground.

'Can I ... Is there someone I can call?'

'I'm okay, really,' Gilligan said. 'I'm parked about five minutes up the road.' He chucked his chin to indicate the direction, and wiped the back of his hand across his drenched brow. He flinched exaggeratedly at the stinging sensation in his arm. He made as if to move off.

The woman, her eyes dropped to his arm, her forehead a frown, told him she had something, and to hang on. He watched her full figure while she leaned into the car, one knee on the driver's seat. The urge to step forward, grasp her with both hands and squeeze her swollen flesh, the way he would test the rump of a Clydesdale, he resisted.

9

She emerged with a bottle of water and a packet of tissues.

Gilligan took them, but made a deliberate mess of trying to open the bottle, as though the cut on his arm had somehow affected his grip.

'My hand,' he said, holding the plastic bottle in the crook of his arm and fumbling to remove the cap. 'I can't bend my fingers. They're frozen.'

'Let me call someone,' the woman said, shaking now in the freezing rain and drawing the collar of her white coat about her neck.

'No, there's no need,' Gilligan said. 'I best be getting on the road. Maybe,' he hesitated and squinted into the darkened road, 'you could just give us a spin as far as my car. I'm just up thataways a bit.'

'But your hand?' the woman said.

Gilligan shook his head. 'Not a problem. All I need is one good hand.' He smiled and held out the supposedly injured one, and curled and opened the fingers on the good one.

The woman looked unsure, but nodded through a clenched expression.

'If, of course, I'm not putting you out?' he said.

'Come on,' she said. 'What am I thinking? It's the very least I can do.'

On the short drive along the country road, the woman talked relentlessly. Gilligan clenched his teeth and bobbed his head up and down without listening. He was going over the scenario he'd practised in his head countless times. But this wasn't that scenario.

'That's me there,' he said, as the woman's headlights lit up his jeep parked at the side of the road.'

'Oh,' she said. 'Right.' And she pulled in behind the Pajero. She flicked on the inside light.

Gilligan could sense her fear now, could almost smell it, and what was flashing through her head.

'It broke down on me,' he said. 'She's been overheating this past while. But she'll be grand now.'

'Good,' she said. 'Good.' She stared straight before her and he could see the way her fingers gripped the steering wheel.

'Any man that raises his hand to a woman, in my books, is not a man,' he said.

'I have to get home,' she said. 'My husband is expecting me. He'll be wondering where I am.'

What happened next Gilligan experienced as though detached from his own being. He might have been seeing things through someone else's eyes.

He reached over, killed the engine, and removed the keys from the ignition. As he did this, the woman sucked in her breath, leaned sideways from him and pushed backwards into her seat. He felt her swollen front press against his arm – the first touch. And then his hand was about her wrist, the other over her mouth. And while he tried to pull her across from the driver's to the passenger seat and into the dark road, he shushed her and tried to reassure her that he wouldn't hurt her. But the woman fought hard and struggled to get out her own door, and alternately clung on the steering wheel, so that Gilligan was forced to give up. Instead, he released her. And while he bustled out his side and ran around the car, she screamed into the night a long scream. That scream he muffled with his large hand, when he grabbed her as she pushed herself from the car.

'Take it easy now,' he said, while he dragged her to the jeep. 'Okay, take it easy. The baby. Think of the baby. We don't want to damage the baby.'

Getting a gag about her mouth proved more difficult than it looked in films, but once he got her hands and feet bound with wheel-ties, he managed to double gag her. Into her mouth he put a piece of torn bed linen. This he reinforced by tying another strip about her mouth to keep it in place.

With the woman safely trussed up and lying in the back seat, a coat thrown over her to keep her warm, Gilligan drove off. By turns, he spoke to her, telling her all about his plans for the baby, or, when he couldn't think of anything worth saying, he raised the sound of Johnny Cash playing on his stereo. He sang along with the song, 'Delia.' In his own voice a new timbre, the triumphant crowing of a rooster when he first hears the cheeping coming from the incubated eggs beneath his favourite hen.

THE STRETCH OF LOVE   ROBYN ROWLAND

For Kuşçu Meral, married to Şerif Ali Ermış, July 27 1991, Bozcaada Island, Turkey

Let yourself be drawn by the stronger pull of that which you truly love. Rumi

When you were young and he said love is elastic
but everything has its breaking point, you decided to stay.
University was another world. He must have been thinking
of fishing-line, being a fisherman from the island.
Strong, it can bear great weight, but if the line is
caught around a rock or the current too fierce, it snaps.
He didn't want to lose you into the wide expanse of
land-locked towns. You felt 'a great love' as yours
would never fail you, but then, his family had the sea
in their blood – being captains – and a fisherman's wisdom.

Now you live surrounded by water on an island of grapes
and flowers, rock and slim soil. You make meals fit for the
table of Rumi whom you love. Fish soup with herbs,
broad bean and artichoke bake, dolmas wrapped in
your own soft grape leaves. Breakfast brings green chilli,
red spices, your olives and their oil, cheeses, tomato, cucumber.
Each day is sweetened with island specialties, tomato jam,
plum, pumpkin, red-poppy jam. Cacao and grape-syrup
cake balance the tannin of essential Turkish tea. Organic,
from your own land, food is the language of kindness.

He built you a tall building, lovely in white and dark pine,
windows to the sea, nautical blue dabbed in corners and alcoves,
a hotel you named Alesta – *ready, prepared, standing by* –
as if she is a boat set for sailing into unknown waters,
taking us along with you. People crowd your bookings.

They come and deliver their tales though evenings of
fluid friendship, then move on breezing into memory.
He brought the world to you this way. No sorrow for lost cities,
journeys not taken, shadow chances. You are precious to him.
He knows the worth in the jewel of you. Knows what you gave.

He gave you Deniz, a son named for the sea, handsome
as the line of island men before him. At seventeen,
one night he returned with his forest of black hair freshly
razed to the scalp. We rushed for dictionaries to translate,
laughing at our stumbling words. At night your love walks with
you along harbour waters to breathe in the best salt-cleaned
air from the Marmara, watch the lights of Turkey bright orange
as pomegranate flowers in his father's trees, arch across the
slick surface of water, nothing to wrinkle its still beauty,
and lifts your face toward heaven's flotilla of stars.

'I WANT TO VISIT THE IMPOSSIBLE GARDEN ...'
PETER STUART-SHEPPARD

I want to visit the impossible garden,
offer you a three hundred year old apple pulled freshly from the
bough,
watch a smile you can't help – as if I could forget
from one century to the next our words and music,
lost and found, held the long moment.
I want to visit the garden
in front of bare trees at Christmas,
lasting through the decades
like a first Timex on the wrist, or the passage of ships
around a blue cardigan, at twenty to three
beside the daylilies.

Such hats we wear! But afternoon beckons like a bowel movement,
my lady –
best not delay. I want to visit the impossible garden,
and wash dishes as we did in the sixties – 1660s, 1960s –
left with our thoughts, our songs, our poems,
the breathings and sighings of water as it rises,
remembering for a moment who we are, whose skin this is, what
brought us here
to this window, as if it was some great accomplishment
we can't quite put a finger on
but brings us to a smile nonetheless, easy now
to tend to what calls from outside –
as if it might be met on familiar terms, and followed.
I want to visit the impossible garden;
perhaps it's the smell of wood that never really dries,
a smell I imagine a trellis of roses would like,
beside the steps and passers-by.

Which door? This? On an old stone wall
a half-eaten apple lies artfully among ivy and moss.
Such winds we've had, but the circle remains intact:
north, east, south, west – we have found them all. Behind you
wren shows a way through the rosehips.
And if I were to say to you, in the bed upon which I sit
that you're beautiful? And if still we heard birds singing?
But a centuries-old darkness has fallen, in front of a yellow street
lamp,
before beams of a thousand candlepower,
leaving my head and shoulders a silhouette against the susurrating
trees – listening,
ghostlike, to moans of cows and marsh fowl plashing in the reeds,
the drone of a moth, looking for light,
streaming past my searching ear, lost
into the house – wanting to visit the impossible garden.

TO THE HUY FONG FOODS COMPANY KAREN RIGBY

Thank you for the plastic rocket on every table
in North America, chilli like rattlesnakes or maracas –
sriracha! – and the dollop of orange
in spicy mayonnaise. For the iconic rooster
to wake my suburban empire of eggs.
Send my regards to Tapatío
and every glass siren at Fry's.
I hear Kettle made sriracha chips,
as did Lay's, and what I need, like a fine haze of powder,
is pain equal to the pain. On the Scoville scale
your sauce rates lower than scotch bonnets,
but good enough for my Chinese/Latina/
Western Pennsylvanian genes.

Last week a Channel 4 English drama
carved verandas in the Himalayan foothills.
Let's talk about colonization for three seconds:
architecture as civilized violence.
Or the sting of my ancestor's rage
when he left a snowbound village
for a serpent republic. On Avenida 4 de julio
shutters close against rain. A peeling balustrade
says nothing of the century's arguments.
Dear Mr. Tran: what's the recipe for global happiness?
Green-tipped bottles ship out of east Los Angeles.
A river of mercury stains my plate.

REMOVAL DAY   COLIN DARDIS

i.m. Tony Dardis

Your hand was always there for the taking,
the request, a tear, fear or basic need.
At six, I cried over what might happen
if you died, the day of our extraction.
The might of imagination, of dread.
Childhood is a voucher redeemable
until the end; and once the ending comes,
let us pray that we can still trade after.

When Charybdis swallows, the port will drain;
the remaining sludge will forever speak
of history. I'll cling to the fig tree
and imagine you docked nearby, waiting.
You cannot pick me up out from the mud.
I cannot lift you up out of the grave.

LINEDANCING   AOIBHEANN MCCANN

The restaurant has black and white photos of men and women in cowboy hats lining the walls. Aileen only recognises Johnny Cash. His picture has a red-lit frame around it. Nancy, the owner, had pointed to it proudly during the interview and announced that Johnny was her Guardian Angel. She said a Feng Shui consultant had confirmed this when they'd taken over the lease. As far as Aileen is aware Johnny Cash is still alive, but she said nothing, she needed the job.

The uniform consists of jeans, a white t-shirt with the logo 'Nancy's Place' emblazoned on a yellow sheriff's badge and a red apron. Thick slabs of steak are served on wooden boards with sharp knives pinning them down for effect. The customers wear shirts with silhouettes of horses on them, suede fringed boots and cowboy hats. Their nasal south London accents clash with their outfits. Knives down, they jump up eagerly from their steaks when their favourite songs come on. Their feet sidestep as they form their fingers into the nuzzles of guns, their thumbs into triggers. They dance in lines like a never-ending soldiers' parade looped on rewind.

Nancy encourages the waitresses to linedance but Aileen prefers to balance the hot plates from the kitchen to the unvarnished tables as when she watches them dance she thinks that maybe Jeff in the flat upstairs is right. He says Londoners are implanted with chips. They've done it in Singapore too, Jeff says, they don't even cross the street at the wrong place there. The Nazis invented the chips, he says, perfected them in the concentration camps. The chips make you obey without question, synchronise your steps with the others. The British government implant people with them to stop them getting crushed at tube stations, he says.

Nancy can't understand why Aileen lives in London.

'Graham wants us to wait until we move to Ireland to have a baby,' she says.

Aileen thinks Graham is a sleaze. In the second week he had stroked the entire length of her arm when she had reached under the hot lamp for the waiting food.

'We're going to bring up our kids simply,' Nancy continues, 'we'll give them oranges and saucepans to play with.'

At night when Aileen goes home she collects Sarah from Mrs Lahiri's, making sure to remember the *Teletubbies* stuffed toy. Sarah grizzles on her shoulder and takes a while to settle after Aileen puts her into the cot. The songs from Nancy's Place twang through Aileen's head, a needle clicking back into the groove playing them over and over. Wailing for lost spouses, mothers and lovers lost through drink and drugs and farm accidents. When Sarah settles she takes the baby monitor upstairs to Jeff's to smoke a joint. Jeff puts on Pink Floyd to repair the damage the Country and Western is doing to her brain.

Sometimes Aileen and Jeff discuss the similarities her life has with the songs. How her lover had left her, though really he had never been to her flat. Croydon was too far out, he said. His flat was in Islington, not a fancy penthouse like she had imagined when she met him, but a tiny one-bed over a launderette in The Angel. There were traces of the other women in the bathroom that she had ignored, a bottle of fancy shampoo in the shower, a single tampon that appeared a few weeks before she last saw him.

Aileen's mother eventually flies over to see them. She insists on coming out to Nancy's Place on the first night, and sits at the end of the bar drinking a Tequila Sunrise. The red and yellow ice sinks slowly through the straw attached to her lipsticked mouth. Aileen introduces her to everyone. They all greet her in their worst Irish accents except for Luca the Italian sous chef. He knows the place of a Catholic matriarch and the respect they demand. By the end of the night after three Tequila Sunrises her mother is giggling hysterically every time they call Aileen Eileen. She sings 'Come on Eileen' loudly on the way home in the cab. The cab driver mutters under his breath about the Irish. Aileen has to put her mother to bed before she gets Sarah. She goes straight up to Jeff.

'I met your mother earlier.' He rolls his eyes and passes the joint before she even sits down. 'I asked what she thought of London, she said it wasn't what she expected it to be.'

19

Aileen nods as she inhales, for once in agreement with her mother.

In the morning her mother is green around the face and doesn't want any breakfast.

'When are you going to go back to your proper job?' she asks, sipping the strong coffee Aileen hands her.

'I'm not going back, Ma, childcare is too expensive.'

She doesn't add that she'd be too tempted to jump under a tube rather than squash back into one. That he'd be there in his office pretending Sarah didn't exist. Sarah screeches from the highchair at the squirrel that climbs up the side of the pebble-dashed alley close to the kitchen window. Her mother groans and goes into the bedroom to lie down.

Another quiet night in the restaurant and Nancy says she'll have to start sending them home early, though she sends Della first. Aileen doesn't talk to Della much as she makes it clear she doesn't think a lot of the Irish. Della had an Irish boyfriend once who drank too much and slapped her a few times. Aileen doesn't tell Della about Sarah's English father, though she can't compare like with like. He never slapped her and boyfriend was too strong a word. Aileen had told him she loved him once. He'd grunted and turned away embarrassed. She had lain awake staring at the orange streetlights while he snored lightly. She hadn't left, as she had known she was pregnant by then. Known she had left it too late for her to have an abortion.

When she was in Mayday hospital giving birth she had screamed for all the drugs they would give her when she finally realised he wasn't coming. He hadn't answered his phone; though he'd made it clear that he wouldn't, she secretly thought he would. That his curiosity or conscience or some primal instinct would get the better of him, or that the dirty looks in the office would bring him there.

Laura from HR had come to visit in the first week with a teddy and some bath bombs from Lush. There was a big card with money in it. Aileen checked the signatures. Laura told her he'd put in £50 though he hadn't signed the card. Laura had rung Aileen the following month to get her to come up to the city for lunch with the girls. Aileen had gone up on the train and the tube, but she'd only got as far as the revolving door of the office.

When the train got back to East Croydon station she'd struggled to get the pram down the narrow steps of the old-fashioned train. No one had even tried to help her. She considered just staying on the train until it reached its final destination, Brighton. Maybe she could pretend Sarah's father was a gay male friend who had obliged her with an empty prescription bottle full of sperm, that she had planned this, that it was a lifestyle choice. She'd stared at the tracks and thought of them going on endlessly up and down this long, stringy country, ending at the sea and turning back in spaghetti loops of time after time of men in suits and women in suits. As she pushed Sarah up the ramp to street level she knew she couldn't ever go back to her old job.

On the Sunday morning shift Nancy is hovering, she already has the music on. This is usually her day off. The smell of scrambled egg is already wafting from the kitchen.

'Things aren't working out,' Nancy says. 'I'm going to have to go back to work in the city. Graham will be doing more of the management.'

Aileen winces.

'It shouldn't affect your shifts though, so don't worry too much. It's just slower than we thought. We'll never get to Ireland at this rate,' she sighs, 'you're so lucky, you can go there anytime, and it's all set up for you, your mother, your friends, somewhere to live.'

Aileen imagines herself back in Sligo, her mother's shame at her clever daughter caught out, now a single parent, failed at London. Aileen's own eternal disappointment at never having had that elusive London life she once thought existed, a Victorian flat in Zone One, or on a tube line at least, dinner in restaurants, wine bars after, VIP entry to clubs, trips to the countryside at weekends, picnics on the South Bank. She knows her life will be the flat in Croydon, shopping in the Whitgift Centre at the weekends and eventually sleeping with Jeff out of loneliness.

Nancy turns up the stereo, they both sing along with Johnny in the empty restaurant. It is Sunday morning and Johnny tells it like it is; lonesome and dead. Nancy walks into the kitchen singing along. Aileen keeps folding serviettes.

MOUNT JEROME   AMANDA BELL

When the summer course in taxidermy
came unstuck, it seemed appropriate
to mark your fiftieth birthday
with another type of preservation:
continuing a lifelong fascination
with the dead, from fruitless excavations
in the bog to Victorian cemetery visits.
To move from Mount Jerome to Père Lachaise
to Highgate would triangulate
your half centenary, confer stability
on the increasingly shaky premise
that anything in life remains unchanged –
that we haven't reached a parting of the ways.
If I had a bag of rounded stones
I'd work them in my hand like beads –
lay them, palm warm, on top of every grave
I visit. The tap of stone on stone –
my calling card – expecting no response
though aiming to connect.
The sharp report more definite
than pots of flowers
or garlands of embellished beads:
each saint's face weathered to a death's head.

LAST CHANCE   CATHERINE EDMUNDS

We're sleeping tonight in the Kitty-Kiss Guesthouse
for the Hard of Eating, experiencing a kind of mean joy,
a last chance for sweary octogenarians. We've brought

no baggage, but are required to state we've found Jesus.
You groan and ache as you lift your lifeless leg to the bed.
We watch it subside. There are things we will never see now,

but still we argue, I claim to know why roads
don't have faces, you shout, you wield words, the hills
swell between us – what a load of absolute horse manure.

I recall when you tasted of salt, when we celebrated
multiple small deaths in Premier Inns. You reckon these days
we both prefer knitting to sex, to free Elvis love songs, a CD

for every reader. King of the clowns, may you reign forever,
but life's a hollow toy, full of panic – a man burns crumpets,
the papers crow. The blood in your eyes compounds your lies.

I demand the fruit, the whole fruit, and nothing but the fruit
now the immigrant loophole through the wardrobe door
has been finally closed. We pull the sheets up

to our noses, listen to our lack of moral fibre.
It's broken. This. You. Me. It. A furious rain falls.
In case of volcanic eruption, listen for mermaids.

THE DEVOURING   PATRICK HANSEL

That December in Philly was so warm
the pruned roses in the backyard bloomed
on Guadalupe Day, and the native shrubs
our teens had planted in the park began to bud.
It was as if all the mortal seeds and tubers
of our life had heard the first trumpet.
At Tacony Creek Park, the shadow
of the red-tailed hawk danced slowly
upon the scrubbed brown earth.
In the brown waters, the long-legged heron
stood watching for a yearling perch.

On Christmas Eve morning, I found a dog
in the park, hind leg broken up, hair mud matted,
eyes like fleas, jumping. We stared across
the waters like enemies, or like lovers,
whose deep secrets were now known across
the great divide of their bodies.
I went back to the church where pounds
of sliced meat past expiration, brought
by Luis from the butchers for the children's
Christmas party, lay in the humming
fridge. They hung, humid ornaments
from my hand, as I returned.

You can walk a path a thousand times
and miss the light it is stealing from the day.
Here was the dog, some ancient pet,
shadowless in the dry ravine where
stormwaters run. To say he was hungry
is to say the earth is round. Or wet.

Or hurtling through space.
I tossed the meat down like a prayer, a flower
floating to earth, the renewal that comes
with dying. The dog jumped back and hung
there, on my sight and on the warm air,
until the devouring hunger in him snapped
his jaw open and he feasted on the salty flesh.

I returned on Christmas, bringing
my seven year old along with the meat,
on the Feast of St Stephen, on St John's
Day, on the Feast of the Holy Innocents.
Each gift of flesh saw his leg straighten up,
his coat soften, his eyes grow mortal
out of the loss he had been thrown into.
My daughter asked what we should call him
and answered before I could speak:
'His name is Michael!' – after her favourite
uncle, or after St Michael, the first angel,
standing watch over God and the creatures
budding from his voice, the sword bearer
the Almighty calls on in battle, the one
falling to earth with Satan in a fight
so fierce, it looks like dancing.

SUNDIAL   NEIL MCCARTHY

Restiveness grants reprieve for your unutterable name,
        exile but a narcissistic luxury.
Waking to a stone against my bedroom window
I see your face, hangdog in the light of the porch.
We hitchhike out to Roundstone under a mussel-blue sky,

the tincture of Connemara barely batting an eyelid
        beneath its westerly spread, the seagulls riotous
in their air of we-know-something-you-don't-know;
the Atlantic a clumsy emissary,
crashing like a brass orchestra down a stairwell.

I take a black and white photograph of you on grey sand
standing like a sundial, back to the camera;
        staring out to sea as if waiting for an allied assault;
or a man holier than I to part the waves and cut you a path
to a belated promised land.

THE SWIMMER   TREVOR CONWAY

The tyres of his bike sprayed a mohawk of water. The rain was cold. It was just a change in circumstances, a slower pace needed. Sligo town didn't look interesting from the by-pass. 'Rosses Point', a sign said, and he slipped away from the traffic.

Coming into the village, he already felt he could write about this place. A small boat was leashed to dry, muddy land where the sea had once rolled. Up ahead, the road rose to a bend, as if offering travellers to the sky.

He set the tent up in the dunes, placed small rocks inside, at the four corners. The rain dribbled to a stop. In the lazy waves below, two arms and a head carved out long, interrupted ripples. This swimmer didn't seem to kick at all. It reminded him of when he first began swimming. The experience of being in the water was all that mattered. Then, exercise. That was the aim. *Progress, always progress*, he thought, and shook his head. He lay on his back in the tent, staring at its dark blue dome.

Ink dimples formed as he pressed the pen to the page. No words. He was drawn to the swimmer. She wore a black wetsuit. Her hair seemed blonde when he looked at her first. But now, he could see there was an orange tint to it, what a bad poet might call 'golden'. She swam towards the next rocky cliff with slow, confident grace. He could write a story about the swimmer, he thought.

An hour passed. He'd written nothing. She'd swum over and back between the two cliffs at least a dozen times, then veered towards the shore. He was surprised at how tall she was, emerging from the surf. Her cheekbones were high, rounded. Out of the water, she had a different kind of grace. She walked with purpose, as though her leisure was over now, and there were things to be done. Sand sprang up and clung to her shin. The path from the beach was only a few feet from his tent. It was rough, but she walked in her bare feet. He looked over as she passed, but she didn't seem to notice.

He'd cycled from Limerick to Sligo over twelve days, and hadn't written a word. He sat looking at the waves. 'She rose from the surf, a giant,' he wrote. Within seconds, he carved a tear in the page, a deep line through the words. He flung his notebook into the gaping mouth of the tent, and began walking.

There were country roads nearby. Most of the fields were empty, but some had sheep or cows. He climbed a gate. It felt like a childish act. He hadn't climbed a gate in over twenty years. He walked to the centre of the field, sat looking at the sky. He hoped some shape in the clouds would ignite an idea. *This field isn't empty*, he realised. There was a ram in the corner, almost behind a tree. It seemed to be trying to run away, held in place by something. He walked closer, and saw that its dirty wool was pressed down by barbed wire.

When he came within five feet, he put his hand out, which only excited the animal. It seemed exhausted, breathing heavily. The ground around it was worn to muck. He pulled lumps of grass up and held it out, stepping forward. The ram's nostrils pulsed as he held the wad of grass near its mouth. It bit in. The power of its muscles were channelled through the tight bundle.

When all that was left was roots, he gathered more and fed it again. He stepped closer as it chewed. It didn't even flinch as he pulled at the barbed wire, which was so tight to its body that he couldn't get his finger under it. He threw the grass down and pulled at the wire with both hands. The ram tried to jump. It let out a long, weary bleat. He stepped back, feeling the sting of a cut on his finger. His heel caught in a root protruding from the ground. He fell back, rubbing his ankle. The ram's bleating was oddly human.

'I'm trying to help you, you stupid fuck,' he said.

When he stood again, the animal seemed nervous. He looked at his finger. There was no blood yet, but it would come.

The nearest house was a small cottage. It was unlikely they owned the field, he thought. There was a large farmhouse a few fields away. One road led him off in the wrong direction, but he found another that brought him to the house. A sheepdog came barking.

'Easy, fella,' he said, opening the gate slowly.

When he stepped onto the path that led to the front door, the dog growled deeper. He noticed a barn to the side of the house. Maybe there were tools inside, and he could set the ram free. He closed the gate, and walked around. The dog leapt over the wall, barking like mad.

He stepped back and looked at the house. There was no sign of anyone there. He'd come back on the bike the next day, he decided.

The wind picked up at night. One of the rocks rolled in his tent. It had two depressions, the size of eye sockets. The image of the ram's skull came to him. He wondered if it had to spend the night standing or whether the barbed wire took its weight. It was riddled with hunger, and all he'd offered it was two fistfuls of grass. Tomorrow, he'd set the animal free. There was a shed over by the car park. Maybe there were tools inside.

He wondered if the swimmer would return. She seemed like the perfect subject for a story. Mysterious. 'All stories start with intrigue,' he once wrote in his notebook. This was the longest period he'd gone without writing. All his early work had touches of death, he recalled. Lying in the tent, staring at this soulless rock, it hit him: his writing began with his father's sickness ten years before. For such a strong man, this word 'cancer' seemed to reduce him. He thought it odd that this had never occurred to him before. His father stopped swimming to save his energy. He didn't speak about the changes happening to him. Maybe all swimmers had some kind of cold, selfish spirit.

His first thought the next morning was of the ram. Maybe the farmer who owned it would notice it was missing. But he expected it had been there for days already, if not weeks. He'd try to do some writing, and if the blank page eyed him for more than a half hour, he'd set off on his bike.

It was just like the other days – not one sentence written. He looked over his shoulder to see if the swimmer was coming. When she came round the bend, she had nothing with her, just her wetsuit. He wondered how far she'd walked in her bare feet.

She got to the soggy sand, opened a zip and took out a silver scissors. She cut off a lock of hair and kicked sand over it. A man with a small dog said something to her, but she marched on without answering. He watched her slip under, barely disturbing the water. He had his first line:

The sea is her blank page.

Was it pretentious? He read it several times. The more he repeated it, the simpler it seemed. It was one of those lines that he knew would endure through several drafts. A word or two might change, but it would stay more or less the same. He watched her surface, taking in air as she drifted on her back. More lines came to him. They didn't seem to be in the right order.

She could tear down these wet cliffs.

She flings out her arms like a boxer fighting from the corner.

With all the agility of a seal, her eyes fixed on the slouching king,
Benbulben mountain.

He slung his jumper over his head and put on his shorts. When he got to the beach, he prised his runners off by the heel and stomped through the shallows. His body barely registered the coldness after a few seconds, kicking and gouging through the water. He kept well away from her path, but veered towards her eventually. He dipped his head under, keeping himself afloat with slow, swirling motions.

She went under again. He had no idea where she was. She came up at the shore. He thought of following her, but just floated there, small ripples wrinkling from his hands.

He made for the shore soon after, dived into the tent and opened his notebook. He wrote so fast that his hand cramped up. He might struggle to make out all the words later, he thought. The sharp shapes of the first page melted into something like Arabic text. At the end of it all, he lay on his side, wet and exhausted.

That evening, he wrote more. And the next morning. He wrote all day for the next three days. Any time he thought of the ram, he was filled with the urge to write. He would go to it when the writing stopped. But it continued. Only meals in the village kept him from writing. He was so engrossed that he barely noticed the swimmer anymore.

On the fourth day, he halted the pen to watch her. At one point, she stopped swimming, suspended in the water. She was looking right at him, he was sure. It lasted no more than ten seconds, and he had no idea what it meant.

Then, the words stopped. It was as if a tap had been turned off. He lay back against the wiry grass. She came out of the water. He watched her disappear round the bend.

In a dream that night, he walked through the field where the ram struggled to free itself. It was still there, standing, now just a skeleton with tufts of wool between the ribs and vertebrae. Its head hung loose. It tried to lift it, but couldn't.

'I forgot about you,' he said. 'I'm sorry.' The pen fell from his hand. The ram made a grunting sound, and lay down.

He woke with tears in his eyes. For the first few seconds, he thought his father was beside him in the tent. He turned on the torch, and decided it was time to leave this place.

He packed everything onto his bike soon after dawn. The shed was padlocked, but the chain was rusty. He picked up a stone and hit it. It took a few minutes to break it. There were plenty of tools, strewn on dusty wooden shelves. He took pliers, a Stanley knife and pruning shears.

When he got to the field with the ram, there were three crows around the animal. He ran at them, but they only scattered a few feet away. He looked down at the ram. Its mouth was open, but its eye moved when he knelt down beside it. He put his hands around its nose and mouth. There was no resistance, barely even breath. And that was soon gone.

He walked away. The smell of the animal was on him. He stumbled to the ground, unable to breathe. The air was cold, like water. He looked up. A wispy cloud hung there. Within a few weeks, the ram's wool would be just as light. Eventually, it would all be blown away. He knew that every time he sat down to write, that image would be somewhere in his mind.

31

DREAM   LAURA DEL COL BROWN

An axiom took flesh and snared him. Turned
To his own diagram, his hindwings bared
In times that called for crypsis, did he move
From panic or from habit? All he knew
Was flight and colour; one no longer served.
He slipped his scales and fled while I still scrubbed
A thread between my pinkie and my thumb.

I dared not wreck the logic of the web
More than I had. I left it for the spider,
Who, met with brilliant dust, would raid her hunger
And spin up substance to repair the wound.
Beauty subsists on beauty; rescue one
And you may starve another; there's your truth,
And much good may it do you on this earth.

GONE, AND OTHERS LIKE HER   ANN HOWELLS

sea numbs, skins heaving planks
we recognize paint that curls from whitish
once whitish flanks, copper eroded keel
salt-spitting slash with every storm

exposed to grey-green water's scour
she steels herself for lingering death
barnacle and worm invade freeboard
gaping ribs hold crab, brine shrimp

wavelets pulse like twitching nerves
microcosms flourish in her fractured hull
buoys sound her death knell
but a heart beats within her cavernous ribcage

age-ruptured, not quite slipping under
what does cant of abandoned deck reveal
salt-caked windows, muck-sunk stern?
sea will not swallow her whole

noon spreads napalm on the shallows
tidal pool mirrors her – pristine
not derelict, not sunk, not salvage
calloused hands once knew her name

LEAVING HOME   SHANNON KELLY

5 a.m. on the Niobrara,
and my father and I pull over
to watch the Sandhill Cranes.

The shock of red above sharp bill,
the hazard-light eyes –
they keep their neck straight

with the precision of a one-room school teacher,
and their feathers are dusted with the grit
of the miles of chalky sky they've crossed.

Imagine the 500,000 of them there,
a swoop of dingy gray bodies huddled
proudly in their scarlet hats, skidding their stilt
legs across the smooth water of the Platte.

These cranes will be gone in a month's time,
veering their long necks out and steering
for California, Minnesota, Mexico.

Rakish, noble, such birds do not cry
at security in an Omaha airport terminal.
Steely-eyed, they take off, send a whoop
across the panhandle sky; these birds dance.

CAULDRON AND DRINK   TIM MILLER

They love their honey and they love the vine,
the wine and beer they engender with fire
and the altered world each takes them to.

They name their vessels like newborns, they name
their goblets and flagons and mixing bowls
and give titles to their cauldrons, those cornucopias

of bronze or clay or silver, a few or
a few hundred gallons deep for meaningful
intoxication and the huge feast,

faces beaten into the metal sheets
polished with running honey and mead and wine:
the gorgon or the boar or the winged deer

or the antlered god, legs crossed, the animal
master with serpent in hand and surrounded
by canine and feline and stag – and so

take a long drink and go for some outsized
strength, go for some feat of appetite and bragging,
drown your faces in grapes, drench your faces in gold.

FADO   MICHAEL SPRING

the Portuguese guitarist soaks
in a bathtub on a rooftop
pours himself another glass
of vinho verde

salutes twilight's last bawling gull
in a sky heavy with clouds

orange earth tones of rooftop tiles
give way to darkening blues of cobbled streets

the guitarist can hear café chairs
scuffling, the alley below
with laughter and voices
and ice clanking in glasses

garlic and salt rise into the belly of air
octopus sizzles on the grill

the guitarist knows it's time to climb out
of this bathwater and tune the strings

tonight Severa will sing fado: a moon
will emerge from the haze of the Tagus river
and the guitarist will become
an enchanted fisherman casting

his interpretation of nets and hooks
into her songs

SOMEONE STANDING IN THE DARK
MICHAEL MCGLADE

Nina sleeps with the bedroom door open because her children have night terrors. It's how she hears the intruder in the hallway.

She left Guatemala before but work drew her back. Thirty-four years old and she doesn't want to die like this, not like this, not when she's finally making a difference.

The intruder pauses in the bedroom doorway shapeless as spilt ink, then clumps his steel toecap boots across the yawning floorboards toward her bed. He wears no mask. Wants her to see him. The whites of his eyes full-moon bright, glossy as hardboiled eggs. He wears a Policía Nacional Civil uniform. Probably one of the Civil Defence Patrols back when death squads operated with impunity.

He leans closer, their faces almost touching now, and stutters hot breath onto her wet skin. He has eaten hotdog. Drank guaro.

She moves her hands onto her naked belly, covers what little she can.

*

Through the kitchen window Nina watches vehicles conga line at a roadblock. Mixed army and PNC on patrol. A daily occurrence. Eight-year-old Jairo and his younger sister Flor are sitting at the breakfast table. He stabs the fried egg on his plate and mops the yolk with a corn tortilla. Flor pastes refried black beans on her tortilla but gets most of it on her hands. Nina wets a dishcloth under the faucet, then remembers the water isn't safe and uses a wet wipe.

'A man came here last night,' Flor says.

Nina moves a wall of black hair behind her shoulder. It's middle-parted like a grade school teacher's, and everything about her features are crumpled as an overworked checkout operator, everything except the hard shots of her espresso-dark eyes.

Jairo says, 'Do we have to leave again?'

*

'Nine years since the ninety-six peace accord. The only thing changing is everything's getting worse. People are poorer now. More Mayan farmers murdered now.'

The telephone line clicks dead.

Nina's morning show on Radio Universidad has no one else waiting on the switchboard to speak. When she started a year ago, there were always too many. But the recent murders have scared them off.

'We have to stop waiting for it all to be better,' she says into the radio mike. 'We have to make it better now.'

She rubs her aching neck.

'Unless we fight for reconciliation through truth, this evil will never leave our country. Our memories – your voices – are the only way to ensure change. These evil people hold key positions in political parties, the Supreme Court, the media. But we know who they are. We'll never stop exposing them.'

A switchboard light blinks with a caller.

'Montt's military attacked my village Dos Erres in eighty-two, looking for Fuerzas Armadas Rebeldes. There were none. We were ladinos, mixed white. A small village with two churches, Catholic and Evangelical. Carlos Antonio Carias, the army commander, gave us a proclamation. Join his Civil Defence Patrol. We refused. Two hundred and fifty were slaughtered, men, women and children. I was twelve. They let me live because I was lighter skinned and have green eyes...'

He stops speaking. Chugs like an engine turning over. The call ends.

Another caller is on the line. She says, 'Nina, what makes you think you can ask us to speak out?'

*

Nina's father dies in an accident when she's nine. He's a university professor. Her distraught mother has five children to provide for.

She's thirteen and in the library. Researching. Nina always asking questions. There's an article about her father that says a death squad entered the college and cut down seven professors, knocking them like bowling pins, and it happened out in the open for all to see. Her father was murdered.

Her mother, traumatized by this incident, has lied all these years. To protect her.

Nina graduates from university with a degree in journalism. She still has no way to get the truth about her father out. She goes to the biggest radio station. For three months she pursues the director of Radio Universidad and gets a meeting.

*

'Some records suggest over two hundred thousand mostly Mayan lost their lives during the civil war. But no one knows for sure. Tell me your story. Truth is our best weapon.'

*

Jose Miguel, editor of *Prensa Libre* newspaper, has thick plummy lips and a solid line of eyebrow across his forehead like it's been drawn with an eyeliner. He is sitting on the edge of his desk, waiting for Nina, his arms folded.

'This article is dangerous.'

She says, 'It's the truth.'

He lifts a printout and reads:

'Since 2001, in just four years, a thousand women have been murdered. Ninety percent have been raped first.'

'I have a daughter,' she replies. 'I don't want her growing up in a world like this.'

'If she ever gets to grow up.'

Nina pulls back her hand to slap him. He doesn't blink but his cheeks redden.

'Maybe I should just run back to the US?' she snaps.

He places the printout on the tabletop. Sucks his teeth while he thinks.

He scans through another article she has sent him.

Civil Defense Patrols. Paramilitary groups. Murders. Control of Supreme Court, customs, immigration, drug trade. Refusal to be dismantled as per the 1996 peace accord. Evidence of terror structures still operating with impunity as they had done during the Civil War. The main difference: instead of acting directly for the state, they now have free reign. Powerful enough to have breached political parties and the media.

'Nina, the fallout will be terrible. To publish it, you must first leave Guatemala.'

*

Nina kisses Jairo's forehead, who is sleeping with his thumb in his mouth. Flor clutches a stuffed lion with one eye missing because he's been through the war. In the hard light of the naked hallway bulb, she watches her sleeping children, their breathing like slow ocean waves.

She steps into the hallway and the rough-sawn floorboards creak.

'I don't want to move again,' Flor says. 'I'm tired moving.'

Nina faces her daughter, who has rolled onto her side.

Jairo says, 'I can stay up tonight and keep guard.'

*

'You have a family,' the caller hisses. 'Do you not worry for their safety?'

'I had to publish the article,' Nina says. 'And I can't keep running. None of us can keep running.'

'What if they take you?'

'They won't,' she says. 'I'm in the public eye. Media attention is keeping me alive. But the people I ask to call in to this show, they're the ones who are in danger. Calling in, telling what happened, that takes courage I don't have.'

*

Nina is at a market stall. 'Licuados en leche. Sin hielo.' The man next to her is staring, watching her and making a point of letting her know he's watching. She avoids eye contact, snatches her fresh fruit shake and rushes off.

The man pursues.

She darts through a gaggle of students. Outside the market, Nina crosses the street, checks the man is gone and takes a breath, having forgotten to breathe. She collides with a police officer and clatters to the pavement. A young couple come to her aid, demanding to know why the officer did this. The officer spits on the ground and sets his hand on his holstered pistol.

Nina springs to her feet and runs.

*

The single-room hut is constructed of bare blocks and has two beds for five people. A single rack of shelves behind a curtain contains everything Nina owns, everything she could grab before fleeing her home. There's a single bare bulb for light and a portable television in the corner with aluminium-foil rabbit ears. The kitchen is outside and has a wood fire. Water for the pila comes from a hose in the street.

Jairo and Flor are playing in the back yard. It's walled in. Relatively safe.

The day after Nina's article appeared in *Prensa Libre*, her radio show was cancelled. Intimidation escalated. Bullets pinged her car.

'I have nowhere left to go,' she says, 'nowhere to turn. I can't go outside because they'll find us.'

Eliseo carries a holstered sidearm and keeps watching out the window, scrutinising the street.

She says, 'You can get me and my family across the border?'

'You have friends here,' he replies. 'We have arranged a meeting with Amnesty International. Maybe they can make you a spokesperson. The others won't dare kill you then.'

*

Lunch is a chicken taco and a pile of shredded lettuce topped with two slices of tomato – all that ever passes for a fresh garden salad. Nina was getting used to it. In the US they had a never-ending array of vegetables but here they were surprisingly lacking. She had been staring at the lettuce for an hour.

'Get the story out,' Eliseo says. 'Same as you always have.'

'But there's no radio station. No newspaper.'

Her hands tremble. Couldn't help but think about her father, how hard it had been to get to where she was, to get her story out.

'You already possess a radio station and a newspaper.'

She glances at the powered-off laptop donated by an anonymous friend. There is no box and the charger is from a different model. Stolen.

*

The first post on her blog is about Nelson Hernández López, an indigenous union and campesino leader murdered on return from a protest march.

An hour later, a reply to the post says:

It doesn't matter if the guerrillas were going to turn Guatemala into another Cuba. Rape, torture and murder of all civilians, whether they supported the guerrillas or not, is indefensible. Montt must be brought to justice and tried for the abominations he carried out on behalf of the state.

Nina receives an email:

Encarnación Quej, indigenous Tzutuhil leader, murdered by masked men on his way to work today.

She broadcasts the news on her website.

More emails.

Gerónimo Ucelo Medoza, leader of the minority Xinca indigenous group, is murdered and five colleagues kidnapped. They are still missing. The group had been demonstrating against mining operations by a Canadian company.

The next day, Nina starts Familiares de Desaparecidos which is a forum in memory of the disappeared. She says, After decades of questions without answers, and a growing list of victims, we create this forum so that the memory of the disappeared will remain. Their stories will be remembered.

She conducts an interview with the *New York Times*:

'Forced disappearance in Guatemala still happens. In fact, it has expanded. And it relies on silent collaboration. It's a means of social control and political dominance which has gained the power of impunity because of the vast political and commercial powers that finance and conceal these crimes.'

*

There's someone outside and the door opens. It's a woman who has come from the protest at Cuatro Caminos intersection. Her head is bandaged with a man's white cotton shirt and there are freckles of blood. She wants to speak about the army killing unarmed protesters. Today it is a friend outside but Nina knows one day they will come for her, same as they did for her father. She will ensure the world knows who they are first.

WHERE DO YOU SEE YOURSELF TEN YEARS FROM NOW?   BOGUSIA WARDEIN

It is 2027 and people celebrate the 110th anniversary
of the October revolution. But I don't recall
if comrade Lenin wore sideburns, though
I am certain the revolt took place in November.
I see myself in Dunnes shopping centre,

on this sunny summer day I wear a long coat
and a woolly hat. Five carrier bags
my constant companions. The biggest one
is a placenta substitute. Smaller ones
contain buttons, beer cans, paper scraps,

which I later scatter around my flat planning
to arrange them in the future so I have something
to look forward to. My collection can be seen
as soon as my door is open by someone other than me.
I am not yet at home. I circle, I sniff, I observe.

All is well as long as children don't run away from you,
said my late best friend. But today they don't pull
the tails of my winter coat. Maybe because of a smell.
I don't worry for it takes six months before a body
begins to stink, and you need to be dead.

What will I do during these ten years besides longing
for today? Walk fast, keep busy pretending
to be busy. Add beer mats, Guinness bottle caps,
plastic containers, well-read newspapers
to my collection of rubber bands in Mason jars.

IMAGINE AN AGING MISS EMILY
LAURA TREACY BENTLEY

basking on a beach towel
with the cupola windows
opened wide to summer's sun.

She's working on her tan,
nibbling at gingerbread,
and sipping Long Island Iced Tea.

Her salt and pepper hair
falls below her waist,
and she sports cateye Ray-Bans

with a matching lime-green bikini.
She paints her toenails bright fuchsia
and etches a perfect em dash

in the middle of each nail.
No one knows
about her lookout hideaway.

If asked, she always blames
her farmer's tan on gardening
without a proper sunhat or work gloves.

She listens to Adele on her iPod
and knows all the words to *Hello* by heart.
When her father takes his long afternoon naps

and her sister weeds the garden
or carries a stepladder into the apple orchard
with a pair of sleepy cats trailing behind her,

Emily unlocks the chest
filled with forty hand-sewn booklets
and reads one poem aloud

until it's burned to memory's dark chamber.
Then she rips the page from its red yarn binding,
cuts it into confetti, and tosses it to the wind.

Silent flurries of letting go,
secret furies of a life unlived.

FOUNDRY   BOBBIE SPARROW

blacksmith I have brought you my steel
formless and wanting secrets in its core

will you place your urgent heat
on this extraneous cool

I want your crucible to temper this rigor

one thousand six hundred degrees
alchemy to reluctance
                    doubt disregard

let flames engorge my silver burden
    melting point release the lie
this weight becoming
            one which I can bear

THE CHRISTMAS PARTY   KATE ENNALS

The sky is a glittering, celestial disco. Neck stretched, I search for Orion with its belt of three stars: Mintaka, Almilan and Alnitak. If I had children, I would have called them after those stars. But I didn't. None of the stars Jack spilled into me took root. He had a low sperm count. Whenever I saw Orion, I thought of my unborn children. They winked at me. Tonight, they were partying with friends. The moonlight was so vivid, I could see my own shadow in the yard.

'Come on, we're late!' I call to Jack. I can see his hunched shape through the kitchen window. It is hard to imagine that this man used to pogo, himself like a shooting star. It was his energy that attracted me. I feel cheated now. Cheated twice.

Living in Fermanagh isn't turning out as well as I expected. People are friendly, but their speech and thought patterns are different. Their words, refrains, and guttural tones come from the bog, the ditches and drains. If I bump into a farmer on the old bog road next to my mother in law's home place, and he starts to chat, I don't understand the half of what he says, something about the dangerous bog holes. I stand nodding and smiling, hoping I'm making the appropriate response. I think they ham it up too. I have an uncomfortable feeling that they are laughing at me.

Jack and I moved here from London when Jack's mother died, and we had to decide what to do with the home place. It seemed a good place to retire. An adventure, I thought. A last stab at life. And I loved the night skies. In London, you cannot see the stars. At first, Jack hadn't been that keen but finally he agreed.

In fact, Jack has slotted in easily. He enjoys the few pints in the pub watching the racing on the big flat screen. Jack likes the fishing too. But I don't fish. When there are village socials, which isn't all that often, the women discuss families. Not having family, I have little to contribute. As I listen to them discuss Sean, Siobhan, or PJ, I am grateful not to have children named Mintaka, Almilan and Alnitak. They would have been ostracised. The gossip goes back generations, literally. Once, I tried joining the men who all stand at the bar, talking football and politics. But they didn't acknowledge me let alone talk to me.

So, this evening I am determined to enjoy myself. We are going to a neighbour of Jack's sister, Sheila, for a meal. I am sure she made him invite us.

Jack comes out. 'Ok, let's go if we have to,' he grumbles. Jack used to be the star of any party but since being here, he seems to have sprouted roots. He never wants to go anywhere. I think that happens when you live in a rural county. There is more of it than you.

We get in the car. I drive and chat.

'Sheila was saying, it's just over a year since Bert's wife died.'

Sheila lives in the village. She regales me with gossip, who did what, when, and how. The characters seem colourful but I often feel excluded. I see myself as an alien, a hairy and feminine 'Extra Terrestrial' figure standing at a gate. Surely, I think, coming from London, a city full of difference and diversity, I should be able to handle Irish rural characters. But here, diversity and difference are of little relevance. I see myself as stuck in my favourite Marc Chagall painting, 'I and the Village'. It is a circle of trapped figures and colour. It was described by one newspaper article as a 'cubist fairy tale.'

'Sheila says there've been a lot of packages delivered to Bert recently. He must be getting into the Christmas spirit! I would have thought Christmas would be a bad time, given his wife dropped dead last December.'

As is increasingly the case these days, Jack says nothing. I pull into the drive. There are three cars here already, and a blue tractor.

'Oh dear, we must be the last to arrive.'

We enter the kitchen through the back door. I know not to knock on the front door. In the first two months, I had stood at the front door, knocking, and no one ever answered. Sheila had laughed.

'We use back doors. I'll take you round and introduce you.'

And she had and I had felt like a prize cow. Well, at least I'm learning the lingo.

In Bert's kitchen, five people sit wearing red Christmas paper hats. A plate of Ryvita crisp bread is spread with pink salmon paste and a bowl of chopped-up hard-boiled eggs are on the table. Quite a tableau.

'Helen, Jack.' People murmur greetings.

Sheila and her husband, Noel, are seated at the kitchen table. Both have their glad rags on. Gerry McGahey, another neighbour, is squeezed into a tightly buttoned grey suit and sits by the kitchen sink. He looks fit to combust. His gnarled fist clutches a glass of beer.

'Just the one I'm having. I've to collect the wife at the end of her hospital shift.'

Bert sits upright. John, his son, lounges against the kitchen presses, in casual wear. Beattie, his daughter, hovers. She wears a white apron spattered with, is it blood stains? She is a wee mite of a thing, ghostly in appearance and character. The garish neon kitchen light casts everyone's faces with a grey pallor.

'Get them drinks, John, and lassie, serve up the food,' says Bert. 'Well, Helen, Jack. Now you're here, we'll go through to the dining room.'

'Will you have a drop of sherry, Helen?' asks John.

'No, Sheila told me Helen likes wine,' said Bert. 'Isn't that right, Helen?'

'Yes, thank you.'

'Jack, you're on the usual? John, get Jack a Guinness. Bring them through.'

'Shame about that Kevin Donaldson, the GAA fella, topping himself,' Bert continues as he takes the seat at the head of a highly polished wooden table. There are cut crystal glasses, napkins and place mats decorated with colourful, long-legged birds.

'They say the boy found him hanging in the pig shed. Not a pleasant sight for the young fella,' says Noel. Beattie comes in and hands round served plates of rice and pork.

'Ooh thank you, Beattie. It looks lovely,' I say, taking the plate. We start to eat.

'Yep, hanging in the pig shed. They're lucky he didn't fall into the animals. There wouldn't have been much of him left,' continues Bert. 'I hope the wine's alright. I don't know much about wine but Sheila said you liked your wine.'

'Lovely. Thank you.'

I lift my glass of red by way of a thank you, and look at the mess of pork on my plate. I think of the body hanging above the pigs. I try to shake the image out of my head. I change the subject.

'So, everyone all set for Christmas?'

'As much as I'll ever be.' Sheila is the only one to respond.

There is more silence. I try again.

'Beattie, are you cooking this year?'

We are all sucking at the dry bits of pork with pineapple that Beattie had served up with sticky rice.

'No,' answers John, 'We're going to my place, aren't we, Da?'

'If you let me bring Tara,' says Bert.

I hadn't heard of a Tara.

'Who is Tara?' I ask.

'The new girlfriend!' Bert laughs. John smiles. Beattie blushes. I nearly choke. This is a surprise. Sheila's head is bent into her plate, trying to prong pig bits.

John changes the subject.

'I see Fitzgerald's place has a SOLD sign up. I heard the young fella lost his job.'

'They say Curran, the auctioneer, bought it himself for a fraction of the cost he sold it to them,' says Gerry.

'Where will they move to?' I ask.

'Tom and the son are going to his folks in Derrylin, Sarah and the girl are going to hers in Ballybay,' says Sheila. 'There's no space in either family home for them all. There's no love lost between Tom and his mother in law.'

'How awful that a family should be split up,' I sigh.

'Money talks,' Jack says to me, in a rather testy way. 'And TJ Curran has never been one to let an opportunity pass, when it comes to investment.'

The table falls into silence again. I feel rebuked. I try again.

'Bert, tell us about Tara.'

'Oh yes, John, will you let me bring Tara?' asks Bert again, while stabbing at a piece of errant pork.

'If you like, Da.'

'Who is she, Bert? You should introduce us,' I say, politely.

'I surely will. We'll join her for coffee and apple pie in the sitting room. This room reminds me too much of Kathleen. She liked to invite the neighbours in at Christmas. But I don't think we're up to it, are we, Beattie?'

In response, Beattie scuttles to the kitchen. The village gossip must be up to ninety. Why wasn't Tara eating with us? Where had she come from? Maybe the village pub had new staff.

'Did anyone go to the Frank McGuinness show in Derrylin?' John asks. 'The seventh son of the seventh son?'

'I heard that he got rid of Francie Stewart's warts, them warts what he's had on his hands all his life!' answers Gerry. 'He's gone around shaking hands with everyone he meets ever since.'

We have all finished eating. Abruptly, Bert stands up.

'Come on, if you've all finished, let's go meet Tara.'

He pushes back his chair. We follow obediently in a procession out of the dining room and down the hall, except for Sheila who goes to help Beattie in the kitchen. I should offer to help, women in the kitchen and all that, but I am keen to meet Tara. Bert throws open the sitting-room door. A small fire is burning in the grate. There are two white leather couches. The room is slick with heat.

'Here we are, Tara.'

Standing in a corner of the room next to the French window is a six-foot blow-up doll, blonde, plastic, smooth, with a shiny sheen. Her lips are pink. She is reflected in the glass so it appears that there are two of her. Drops of condensation on her upper lip make her look lusty.

'She's great company altogether,' Bert says, rubbing his hands. 'The best gift of a woman a man could have. Come in, come in. Beattie will bring coffee and tart. Merry Christmas, everyone.'

'She's a doll!' I exclaim.

'She surely is,' said Bert. 'What were you expecting, Helen?'

'I don't know. A woman, I suppose. I mean, what do you do with a blow-up doll?'

The men look at me. My face burns. I put my hand up to my cheek.

51

The room is unbearably hot.

'I heard that seventh son also cured Johnny McCann,' said Jack, winking at Noel. 'You wouldn't be having that sort of trouble now, Bert, would you?'

I was grateful to Jack for changing the subject. I sit down next to him.

'What sort of trouble is that, Jack?' I ask.

'Not any kind Tara will know about,' said Noel.

The men laugh. I squirm. Beattie arrives with the coffee, puts it down and scurries out.

'I'll help Beattie in the kitchen,' I say. But I don't go to the kitchen. I step outside, and look up into the night sky, still studded with stars, grateful for the cool air. The cubist fairy tale is closing in on me. I look up. I feel the tug of space and emptiness. What am I doing here? I feel desperate to join my babies. I feel for the car keys in my pocket, get in the car and head towards the bog.

HOW SHE SPENT HER LAST DAY   OJO TAIYE

there are languages for loss, I know them all
my mother is incontinent & the July air is humid
mother's milky blue eyes no longer see
but open at the sound of an unfamiliar voice
she no longer worries about how life smells,
if she breathes in too deeply all she tastes is ash

I sit on the bed & take her hand – a blue vein pulses
through her old skin which ripples over prominent bones
her palm is cool & dry, her breath struggles like the
last flame of a dying fire

at dusk when bats skim the half-light for insects
my father says: your mother needs rest now
kiss her goodnight & wait for me in the garden

mother's garden is fragrant with shrubs & flowers
attracting nectar-hungry butterflies & bees
I close my mother's world & breathe in the lingering
scent of lavender & Buddleia bushes, flower-heads
drooping like bunches of purple grapes

looking back at the house where mother's room is now dark
I wait for the wailing & the sound of grief to begin
but the house remains still & silent
I rip my shirt above my heart: a ritual for moths
there are marks on my chest, letters written in black ink
with my fingertip I trace the names that cover my skin

160 EAST 48TH STREET   CHRISTINE VALTERS PAINTNER

'(T)he house we were born in is physically inscribed in us.'
– Gaston Bachelard, *The Poetics of Space*

Sometimes at night
I am there again.
Midtown Manhattan,
all concrete and spires and sirens,
funnelled along stone alleyways
by blinking
red, yellow, green.

Doorman sentry
allows me passage,
witness to arrivals and leavings.
Twelve stories up in the elevator,
that feeling of going aloft
to our home suspended in air,
still carved in me like a whisper.

Our living room, with the
Chrysler building view
vanished on foggy mornings,
and the sea of brick-framed
windows thick with city-grime,
all those lives labouring
ferociously behind them.

There is the dusty metal tray
in the kitchen with half-drunk
bottles of scotch and vodka,
and the smoke rising

in silver curls from the ashtray
there on the plastic-covered table,
the window cracked open.

Fire ambulance wail heralds
some nearby suffering.
A pigeon lands on the sill,
in a world full of clamour
its cooing comes like
a quiet annunciation.

UNHAPPY MEALS   JOHN REINHART

you hear the stories;
they're all true:
don't eat the food

the stories of lost souls,
lost memories, lost hopes,
lost chances, lost divinity

don't eat the food

if you get dragged down
into the underworld,
hoodwinked by some trolls,
tempted by riches or beauty,
promised lifetimes of luxury
or the chance to win a weekend getaway,
don't eat the food

no matter the advertising –
gleaming pomegranate pips,
succulent red apples,
raspberries ready to explode,
mammatocumulus mashed potatoes,
sparkling crisp chicken fingers –

don't eat the food

it's not worth a lifetime
or an eternity stuck in the void,
in service to some otherworldly being,
chained to some rock
while eagles make their own meal,

convenience, marketing, or long lines
of hungry people must not convince;
such contrivances are illusion,
and it's a sorrowful god
who stoops to the golden arches
or the promise to eat the burgers
of kings – don't eat the food

picture Thor on the couch
screaming at the TV for more touchdowns,
beer belly pushing the remote buttons,
Mjölnir in the garage under a neon sign

or Rama stocking chicken soup
on the graveyard shift while Shiva
rings out customers, eating donuts
under the register

or Isis and Osiris shoe shopping
at the mall, Loki hawking fake Rolexes
in Times Square, while Athena repairs tractors
outside Des Moines, Ishtar
heads a brothel in the Nevada desert,
and Hades waits
at the drive-thru window:
'You want fries with that?'

THE TOURIST   BENJAMIN SMITH

A film star from the seventies.
The faint scent of yesterday
on pale yellow wallpaper. Two

bars of soap, a towel, a razor.
A foreign face, foreign hands.
The faded memory of a name

from miles back. Numbness.
A hole in the wall where light
cascades. A portrait of a man

alone in a room. A brass band,
drunk, far out at sea. Fireworks.
Someone else's birthday party

on tv. A disoriented rain-dog's
wounded bark, a car trailing off
into the distance. Warm water,

soap, a razor. A shot of tequila.
A hole in the wall where light
cascades. Fireworks. The sunrise.

SIR   JUSTIN ALLEN

My girlfriend Paula, who lately I've been fantasising about murdering, went to Half Moon Bay with me last weekend. I hate these little coastal towns in California, the bland prosperity they exude, the ridiculous nautical trinkets in the tourist shops, the predictable modernity of chic eateries precisely calibrated to make it effortless for the tech worker to throw away their money by the hundreds. The weather is usually grey and cold, no matter what time of year, anywhere north of Santa Barbara.

Paula had picked out a restaurant in advance on Yelp as I drove. We sat drinking chilled white wine, eating excellent seafood, and had nothing to say to each other. This is what we had come here to do, aside from wandering the small streets and presumably, engaging in some other consumer activity, supporting the local economy by purchasing some obscene object such as a porcelain fishing hut hand-painted by a Chinese slave labourer to resemble a fucking Thomas Kinkade painting. There's always options when it comes to consumption: instead, if we wanted to spend money like the thoughtful, progressive class of wealthy people that we are, we could buy a set of windchimes made out of reclaimed metal from a condemned barn by an unemployed Burning Man devotee with a heavy marijuana habit.

I quickly finished my linguini, along with several glasses of white wine, and sat absorbed in my iPhone as Paula finished her meal. Feigning interest or enthusiasm was more than I could handle, and she knew better than to push. Everything else, I could manage – but not that. When the server asked us if we cared for dessert, I curtly said no. Paula looked dejected. For this, I apologised: 'I'm sorry. I just have to get out of here.'

She sighed. She gazed down at her plate, then back at me.

'What's so horrible here, anyway? What's wrong with it?'

This threw me off a little. I didn't really know how to explain.

'Nothing,' I said. 'I'm just tired of sitting here.'

'But you couldn't wait to stop walking around. You wanted to go to the restaurant.'

'Did I?'

I honestly had no recollection of this. But that was normal, if unsettling every time. My short-term memory was bad and getting worse. It was as if I had blown some mental fuses while programming, and in my analog life, was now operating with impaired functionality.

'You did,' Paula said, solemn, her voice full of reproach. Haloes of light shone from the glasses onto the white tablecloth, and I had the passing urge to slap her across the face. Just a thought, really, one which I would never act on. It was one of those things. I felt trapped by Paula, by her dependency on me. She had her own job, though it paid half what mine did, and she certainly enjoyed the bourgeois San Francisco lifestyle my tech career afforded us, so there was, no doubt, the old-fashioned kind of dependency. But it was the emotional dependency that kept us locked in a death spiral; she needed me to focus her frustrations on.

She was not alone in this. When I looked within, I could see that I was, as well, totally dependent on her: not simply as an object to funnel my hatred of life into – that was true enough, but I spread that around. Even more, as an element of my existence which, like my programming career, I felt I had chosen poorly but was now stuck with, too late to change. Any effort to change would only leave me worse off, in a different and even worse trap than before. In any case, I could never leave. Hence, my violent fantasies, when we found ourselves at the top of long stairways or when I was driving and thought of giving a sudden twist to the steering wheel. Like that very day, in fact, on those death-defying cliffside roads with soaring views of the ocean.

There's a unique kind of exhaustion suffered by the programmer: the brain buckles under the sheer amount of syntax it has to absorb. Rivers, floods of character patterns: curly brackets and square brackets, parentheses, forward and backslashes. Seas of variables, nested abstractions one must trace back, and back, and back, to unravel exactly how the program works. Complex patterns, flowing by so fast you can never pause enough to fully comprehend them all, but must maintain some surface level of awareness of, because inside that ocean of punctuation there are snags, knots, trapdoors – that will someday confound you, maybe drive you to the limits of frustration.

After we left the restaurant, we walked down the main street of Half Moon Bay. The sun was setting, and it was a beautiful and eerie twilight, red gold at one edge of the sky, and dark, threatening blue at the other. We came in sight of a small plaza I'd seen earlier, with some tables where Latin American immigrant men gathered, killing time and waiting for someone to hire them. I supposed that many of them were homeless, and had nowhere to go.

As we approached, I could see a police officer get out of his squad car, the lights silently spinning, and walk up to a brown-skinned man curled up in a sleeping bag under a table. It reminded me of when I used to sleep at the office under my desk, back when I was a pretentious boy genius flouting office convention. Before I'd realised those kinds of theatrics just raised expectations. We kept advancing, though Paula slowed, started drifting behind me. The cop was saying something to the immigrant. A blip of static burst from his radio, betraying his cyborg nature: the cop was a mere node on a network, a program written by somebody else, many layers of abstraction above.

Then, the cop kicked the immigrant. To be fair, it was not a hard kick – it was almost a nudge, presumably to wake the sleeping vagrant. All the same, the naked expression of power was too much for me. My mind raced with images of police brutality, police murder, that I'd seen on the Internet.

'Hey!' I shouted.

The cop turned and looked at me.

'Why don't you leave that guy alone?'

I walked right up to the cop – clearly, in retrospect, too close. He was shorter than me. Shaved head, thickset. A big, potato-shaped nose. In short, a very unattractive person, and very unhappy-looking.

'Who's he bothering just lying there, anyway?' I said, full of indignation. 'He's just lying there sleeping!'

The cop was dumbfounded.

'Step back, sir,' he said. 'Step over to the sidewalk.'

He pointed, with that trademark patriarchal authority, toward his squad car. Paula was standing nearby, terrified.

'No!' I shouted. 'You can't just issue me commands. You're a public servant. You answer to me!' I thundered, pointing at my chest.

Me!

I was the Master!

I was the Master of this cop!

The policeman blinked. This was almost working.

'What's your badge number!' I demanded.

The cop calmly took out his radio and spoke into it, looking right at me without blinking. He said, as I watched him with my heart pounding, that he had a 'drunk and disorderly man accosting him' and requested backup. I then turned to leave. But the cop was just getting started.

'Proceed to the car and stand by it, sir,' he said.

It occurred to me – I remember thinking exactly this – that the way police use the word 'sir' is a perverse inversion of that word's conventional meaning. 'Sir,' which always conveys social distance, is usually an honorific implying respect, even nobility on the part of the recipient, and servility on the part of the person using it. When a cop calls you 'sir,' though, you'd better watch out – what they mean by 'sir' is something like a pure reversal – something more like 'subject': an objectified human disconnected from their social context on which the instrument of authority is prepared to exercise power to enforce the social order. Which they are permitted – no, encouraged – to use violent means to maintain.

I then said in my entitled way, 'Paula, let's go,' which was a downright comical gesture, because directly after I said it, swerving to walk away from the squad car, the cop, anticipating I'd do exactly that, put one practised hand between my shoulder blades and another on my arm and forcefully propelled me to the squad car. A moment later, I was sprawled on the side of it, after having stumbled and fallen into it, hugging it to keep from going completely down onto the concrete. I'd slammed my face into the car hard enough to bust my lower lip open, and could instantly feel the hot blood dribbling down my chin and onto my shirt. The cop hoisted me up, wrenched my arms behind me and put cuffs on me. In another moment, I was in the back of the police car.

I craned my head around and could see, in the flashing light, the cop talking to Paula. Her face was pallid, twisted into a terrorised apology. She was talking. Her hands were clasped, as if in prayer. The cop's bald head was nodding. His hands were planted on his hips. He was the Master now, he had the power. I looked back at the plaza and with a rush of adrenaline and sense of triumph unlike any I've felt in my life, I saw that the man with the sleeping bag was gone. He got away. My act had not been meaningless. So really, it didn't matter what happened now.

CAUSEWAY   MAUREEN HILL

A mile of rugged gravel takes us down
groups tatter talk fades out
heavy mewling sky oily sea
honeycomb of blank grey blocks,

I strive to be amazed
clutch at textbook facts –
140,000 hexagonal basalt columns, volcanic, 60 million years ...
seek comfort in domestic myth,
a giant hurling stones, a pathway to a rival ...
take obligatory selfies against the view,
head off alone, to stare and stand, commune.

Some tick of anxiety is plucking at the edge of thought,
a subtle change of light,
a delimning, an unravelling begins.

The man beside me is now a scaly sea creature
flailing on the dry stones,
my own soft flesh is locked in carapace,
around me crustaceans scramble,
slow to a sepia freeze-frame, fade.

The hexed columns are humming to themselves,
some proto music before sound,
huge organ pipes of silence fronting infinity,
petrified fire and flow.
I am walking into the absolute of blind rock,
my thoughts are a scrannel of pebbles at my feet,
I am stunned out of time, stoned,
fugued to nothing,

uber utter utmost void.

A flurry of movement and murmur,
the yellow Disney bus is coming down the hill.
We head for it, twittering like gathering birds,
glad to be going up
back to car park, coffee, trivia,
I resist the vague sense of some happening –

nothing happened,
we have been to the causeway. We have seen it.

POVERTY 1840   REBECCA GETHIN

That was the day the babby became Button.
When I handed her over
I gave the lady my last one as a token,
knowing I'd be back for it.

The babby was becoming unstitched from me,
like a button loosening and if I could
I'd have stitched her firm
so she'd not dangle and fall

from the worn jacket of family
but months ago I used up
the last of the thread
and my needle turned rusty.

Note: tokens were left with babies given up to the Foundling Hospital.

BULSARA — PATRICK CHAPMAN

Powerless to walk, you were helped
to the limousine that carried you
to Harley Street back doors,
eluding the wolves who
called you gaunt.

Having all the 'fuck you'
money in the world,
you blessed your
dears with
homes –
and how your future spirit must
have grinned for minutes at a
time in the booth as you laid
a trove of vocals down
to finish the band.

These days you appear where
your ghost light never dims,
to whisper *a capella* arias
in brokenhearted
boudoirs.

She is waiting in the porch when he pulls into the driveway.

'I have to pop to the shops for some bits. Breast pads and stuff, look at the state of me,' she says. He gazes at her chest. At the two damp patches on show through her red polo-neck.

'I could've got them for you,' he says. 'Why didn't you ask me?'

'They're special slim ones, I've forgotten the name of them. I'll know the box when I see it,' she says, pulling her denim jacket on and hooking the copper buttons at the waist. She can no longer close the ones higher up, much as she'd like to. She knots her black scarf over the gap instead.

'How long will you be?' he asks as she slides the baby's car seat onto her arm.

'An hour or so,' she says, turning her back to him so that he can't see what is happening to her cheeks. That infuriating, tingling burn. As if she's done something.

'Which shopping centre are you going to?' he calls after her.

'Don't know yet,' she shouts back, fiddling with the belt around the car seat. Glad of the darkness of early winter taking the heat out of her face.

She backs out of the driveway and waves at him, at his silhouette, motionless, lit by the lamp in the hall. As she drives up the hill and away from him she realises she has left her phone behind. She brakes. Then she presses her foot back on the accelerator, filling the road with a plume of smoke. On down the by-pass she goes, a little more quickly than she should, until she's stopped by some temporary road works. She fiddles with the radio before deciding to leave it off. Then the man in the neon yellow-jacket turns the sign from *Stop* to *Go* and he winks at her. She takes off, passing her usual shopping centre on her right. The street lights along the sea road seem kaleidoscopic, twinkling, pulling her along as if in a tunnel. Pulling her all the way into town.

Grafton Street is thick with late-night early Christmas shoppers. She ducks and dives her way through, as her baby's eyes dart around like E.T.'s. The little legs dangle from the sling and seem to jig about as they approach a lone violinist. She stops.

'Vivaldi,' she shouts out, as if he is there with them, quizzing.

What movement though? she hears him say.

'Vivaldi's Four Seasons,' she whispers now.

Which one?

'Spring,' she tells him.

Good.

Bewley's cafe is just ahead and she can smell the coffee beans roasting and being ground. A smell that tells her she is really in town. She decides that's where they'll go after picking up the bits from Mothercare in the Stephen's Green Centre.

She can't find them at first. The special pads. A multi-coloured polka dot gro-bag has caught her attention when a shop assistant appears in front of her.

'Ah, God, how old?' the assistant asks, smiling into the sling.

'Three months,' she says, pulling the baby's crochet knit hat back.

'She's taking it all in, anyway,' the assistant says.

The baby begins to whimper.

Anyway.

'I'm looking for those slim breast pads you stock here,' she says, feeling the milk ooze out of her, responding to the cries.

'I don't want to look any more stuffed than I already am,' she says, trying to laugh.

'Follow me,' the assistant says. She looks at the assistant from behind. At how young she seems. Tiny. Shoulder-length silky blonde hair. If it wasn't for the black uniform she'd be mistaken for a child.

'These ones?' the assistant asks. The cries are becoming piercing now. She is drenched with fresh warm milk.

'Yes. God. The baby needs a feed,' she says feeling out of her depth, her cheeks beginning to tingle like they do for him. It was wrong of her to come all the way into town, she thinks now. A stupid, stupid thing to do.

As the assistant looks up at her, she notices that her large round hazel eyes are flecked with gold. All around the pupils, like mini-sunflowers.

'Follow me,' the assistant says, again, and she leads her to the back of the shop.

'You can feed her in there,' she says, pointing into a small dark room with a cream-cushioned armchair in the corner. Deep red carpet on the floor.

'The bulb has gone,' the assistant says, 'but we can prop the door ajar for a bit of light. No-one will disturb you,' she says and she's gone. There's no chance to even thank her.

She unhooks the sling and wriggles the yowling baby out of it. Then she sinks down into the chair, positions the mouth onto her left nipple, feels the let down reflex kicking in and the milk beginning to gush. Spraying out of her as the baby pulls away. It's coming too fast for her and her latch isn't great. Better than what they were told it would be, but not great. She catches some of the spray in her hand before re-positioning the mouth. She licks the milk from her palm. The sweetness of it surprises her, as if it has been honeyed somehow. The speed of it exiting calms down as the baby finds her rhythm. It oozes out of the right breast though. Fresh milk onto the stale stuff hardened in her bra from earlier. This is what she's thinking about as she sinks further down into the chair. *Fresh. Stale.* Words spinning in front of her, spinning and spinning until she closes her eyes to stop them.

It is some time later when the baby lets out a squawk and she opens her eyes into the dark, dark room. It takes a moment or two before she works out where she is. As it hits her, the realisation of what has happened, she waits for the panic to take hold.

We are locked into a shop in a closed shopping centre.

She whispers this, over and over, expecting to hear her heart thumping, or to feel her windpipe constricting. Nothing. Nothing happens at all. Creeping out of the little room, she surveys the shop.

'Hello?' she calls out softly.

Then she carries her sleeping baby over to the Moses baskets. There's a display one all made up and she pops her baby into it. She takes her boots off and walks around the shop to see if it will set off an alarm. When it doesn't she feels her ribs relax down. The shutter is pulled over the door but the large windows are catching light from the main shopping centre. Security lights for the night. She can see enough to select what she'll need. A twin cot and lots of baby blankets. Lime green and yellow she chooses and tosses them into the cot for later. She does not need sleep yet. For now she stands and listens. Listens to the silence. Listens to him not quizzing.

The leaked milk that has dried onto hardened earlier spillages has lost its sweet smell. The sourness reeks through her and stiff material is chafing her chest. She wonders about it now too. If old spillages can go off and make her baby sick. Taking herself over to the maternity clothes section she picks a new white feeding bra and a turquoise wrap-around nursing top. As she strips there in the middle of the shop floor, she catches a glimpse of her nakedness. The distorted breasts do not seem to belong to her. It's as if she's at a funfair in the house of mirrors trying to give herself a fright or a laugh. A siren blasts out on the street. She hooks the bra together, swivelling it around and quickly covering herself. The new material is instantly soothing. The nursing top has an alarm tag on it. Bringing it over to the cash desk she fiddles with the tag, shoving it into what seems to be the de-tagging device. She cannot make it work, no matter which way she pushes it, it will not release. The muffled sound of men's voices warbling *Wonderwall* seeps in. A stag night, she reckons, as she gives up on the tag.

A green light flashes on the desk phone. She could pick it up and call someone, she supposes. But who? He will be the only one who is looking, frantic. She thinks about the stroke of luck she had leaving her mobile behind. Otherwise he'd be using his iPhone tracking app to locate her. He'd be able to see with his Life360 exactly where she is. A little box with a smiley face and arrow pointing directly into the Stephen's Green Centre. If he's using it now it will tell him she's at home. Just as she should be. Her

71

cheeks crease into dimples now as she thinks about this. She leaves the nursing top covering the phone and with goose bumps springing up on her arms she goes back into the little room for her jacket. Sitting back down in the cushioned chair she thinks about this time last year when her best friend Suzie crashed at her house after the school reunion. The next morning they're trawling over the night. Counting the kids and the break-ups of their classmates. She's making a hard-boiled egg and toast for him while Suzie flushes herself with Panadol. She lays the table, puts his egg, toast and a plunger of coffee ready for him and sinks back down on the couch.

Where's the black pepper? he blurts out.

I think we're out of it, she says.

You know I can't eat an egg without black pepper.

Suzie giggles, louder and louder. She thinks he's joking. Then he stands up and hurls the egg across the room, the shell smashing into smithereens as it hits the kitchen sink tiles. Then it bounces onto the draining board and down onto the floor.

She knows it then. But the pregnancy announces itself, the blue cross springing up saying of course, of course, now, and she weeps when she sees it. She weeps and she tells herself that it will be fine. A baby is just what they need to make it all fine.

The baby lets out a sharp shriek. She runs to her, plucks her from the basket and whispers as a torch flashes through, flickering off the safari play mats.

'Shush now, I've got you,' she says, and she's down on her knees crawling with her baby past the row of buggies and back into the little room to feed again. Feeding beautifully with her split gaping mouth.

I thought you took your folic acid, she whispers now. His words when he saw.

The baby's mustard yellow poo has shot up her back and is leaking through her white baby-gro. She goes back out onto the shop floor, pulls a changing mat down from the shelves and then plucks a packet of new-born vests. She stares at the selection of baby-gros, at the pale pinks of the girls' section before choosing from the boys' section instead. A midnight blue one with a train on it. She changes her and puts the nappy along with the soiled suit into a nappy sack and back into her bag. Then she climbs into the twin cot, curling herself into a foetal position, cradling her baby.

The rattling of the shutters from the shops around, announcing opening time, does not startle her. She is ready. She has left a 50-euro note on the cash desk. She stands in the little room with the baby sleeping on her. There's a screech as the Mothercare shutter opens. She counts. Sixty seconds. Then she slips out of the room and winds her way around the shop as if she has just come in looking for something.

THREE WAYS OF FALLING   KRISTIN CAMITTA ZIMET

I

All praise for gravity, for this clay body turning into slip
on the soft mattress. I am a fallen oak sunk in a bog,
soaking up minerals, finding its density, its rings of stone.
My skull unplugs, hollows, an open urn. My mind slides
gravel embankments, slumps in the water table, settles in
under the O horizon. Words slough into sleep.

II

All praise for gravity, for the centripetal pull of the whole
against the outward rush, a thousand starlings peeling off a tree,
splashing the sky. Under these blankets, under the press of age,
I draw them back. Skittery loves and stratospheric voices
bump down in twilight, curling scaly feet around the branch.
Mine is the chest, the cave in which they keep.

III

All praise for gravity, for love's insistence quickening a disc
from interstellar cloud, soul from imagining, coaxing
the gravid belly to bear down, firming the fontanel.
Now I am falling like a meteor, closing on earth's
rough shining. I need the furnace at the very core.
Curl me into your centre. Take me deep.

MERROW   SURI PARMAR

In the wake of a brief but respectably torrid love affair, Tally hopped on a plane from Toronto to Ireland, hoping, like so many others, that crossing an ocean would moor the loose ends in her life. After all, new surroundings signal new beginnings.

In Ireland, she felt all the more adrift. When she tried befriending locals in Dublin – at pubs, on the street – she was called an 'ignorant American.' ('I'm Canadian,' she responded.) Towns like Dingle and Killarney were tourist traps more suited for families and honeymooning couples. Nor did she take to the coast, with its craggy, almost comically lugubrious beaches. Compounding her misery, Ireland was experiencing its coldest, wettest summer in years.

Nothing had prepared her for Galway.

The rest of Ireland mocked her solitude. Galway, though, was unsettling. On the bus, she'd flinched entering the city. The crumbling stone buildings, quaint bistros and teashops bridged with bunting, pubs and hostels bursting with exuberant backpackers. It all seemed so calculated, like a movie set. Splitting the city in twain, the River Corrib wended into Galway Bay, still and grey beneath a colourless sky. Who knew what secrets its depths harboured?

She had a mind to leave Galway and fly home early. Back to the life she'd fled. But her credit cards were nearly maxed out and she couldn't afford to change her flight. For the first two days after arriving, she kept to her hotel room, ignoring her mother's phone calls and emails demanding to know if she was all right, streaming movies on her laptop, and uneasily staring outside at the river. It watched her.

Eventually cabin fever got the better of her. On the third day, after showering and eating a quick breakfast, she resolved to explore the city. The weather was unseasonably warm that morning; she didn't bother with a raincoat or wellies.

By noon, she had wandered to the Spanish Arch: a gated segment of stone wall near the mouth of the river. It was a lively scene. An outdoor market was in full swing: potters and artisans hawking painted clay vases and ceramic picture frames. Some vendors sold cakes and scones, and single-serving jars of jelly and clotted cream. Threading her way through a maze of white canvas awnings, Tally bought a cheese scone and sat away from the crowds of tourists, at the far end of the market on the Long Walk quay. She leaned against a bollard, trying not to notice people walking hand in hand.

She withdrew a can of tuna she'd bought at a grocery store from her purse. Most meals during her travels had come from a tin. Restaurants were out of the question, the Canadian dollar was so low, and moreover, Irish meals were too heavy for her liking. She pulled back the can's foil lid.

Inside was a lump of bloody blue flesh.

She cried out. With shaking fingers, she checked the can's label. Shoal's White. A regional brand, well before its expiry date. Disgusted, she prepared to toss the mess in the river, but the Corrib's clean waves glinted at her reproachfully.

Looking closer, she saw that the meat was veined with spidery markings that resembled runes. Grey, no, silver runes that seemed to emit a faint humming noise. Which was impossible – it had to be the wind blowing. A smell hit her nostrils. Sepulchral, with a not unpleasant undertone.

Salt. Sand. A hint of iodine.

The humming grew louder. She closed her eyes, recalling a childhood trip to Vancouver Island. Wading in ocean shallows, sea slime staining the soles of her feet. Her father lifting her onto his shoulders and carrying her into the water as she shrieked with gleeful terror. She inhaled once more – deeper, this time – and felt the tightness around her chest ease. Just a touch.

Then there was a crash, followed by keening.

The humming ceased. Tally looked up. A nearby booth table had collapsed; its end obscenely jutted into the air. A woman in a weatherproofed poncho was crouched over cobblestones, scrabbling at heaps of ceramic shards. 'Three thousand euros down the drain,' she sobbed, strands of auburn hair escaping her bun.

Her eyes, red-rimmed and accusatory, met Tally's. Tally looked away, feeling guilty for some reason. She wrapped the can in a plastic bag and stuffed it in her purse, out of sight. Rising, she shielded her eyes as the Corrib flashed in the sun. It was laughing.

A crowd formed around the woman. They carefully stacked the broken wares, cooing and soothing, but she was inconsolable. As Tally walked back to her hotel, the woman's wails filled the air, mingling with the sounds of the river.

*

'You sold me bad tuna.'

The cashier at the grocery store smirked as she glanced inside the can. She was an older woman with dark sunken eyes and wind-stung cheeks, a languid air. 'That's not tuna, love.' She plucked the can from Tally's fingers and dropped it into a wastebasket.

Tally's voice spiked with frustration. 'I could have been poisoned.'

'Oh, I doubt that,' the cashier said, wiping her fingers on her apron. 'Sick as a dog, mayhap, and never the same, but not poisoned.'

'Aren't you going to offer me a refund?' The cashier shrugged and dropped a few coins on the counter, which Tally irritably pocketed. 'What do you suppose it is then, if not tuna?' she couldn't help asking.

'Who knows what them fishermen snag in their nets? Dolphin, seal. Merrow.' Tally looked at the cashier, bewildered. 'Mermaid,' the cashier clarified, tucking a wispy red curl behind her ear. 'The Corrib's thick with 'em.'

'Wait. What –'

But the cashier had turned to the next customer in line. 'Can I help you, love?'

*

'Merrow,' Tally said.

It was late afternoon. The sun was low in the sky, wreathed with silvery clouds. She was sitting on the Long Walk, having returned every day since the marketplace incident. Watching the water closely, she maintained a riverside vigil. To what end, she had no idea.

The Corrib's thick with 'em.

What had the cashier meant? She must have been joking. Surely mermaids didn't exist. Tally knew she was being ridiculous. Did she expect to see Ariel from the Disney film swimming in the river?

Idly, she rubbed her shins. Her legs were acting up again. They had felt stilted these last few days, leaden, almost dissociated from her body. Perhaps dampness had settled in her bones. She would visit a clinic – after all, she had bought travel insurance. She imagined doctors sawing off her legs and hurling them into the Corrib.

Or she could push through whatever was ailing her and go back to her hotel. Dress up, get spangled at a pub like any other tourist. Have a holiday fling. And then what? Return to Toronto, to her cramped one-bedroom apartment, the office job she hated, a dating pool teeming with ditchwater-dull men? There was nothing for her back home.

Then she saw it.

A face in the waves. Blue skin, framed with wet, lacy strands of reddish-brown hair.

Tally looked around, her heart quickening. Had anyone else noticed? No. People continued strolling along the walk, happily, jauntily oblivious. She must be out of her mind.

An hour later, she was rewarded with another sign. A spreading fishtail that rose from the water, about twenty metres from where she sat. Thick and scaly. Backlit by the setting sun.

Nobody else saw it. This time, Tally didn't care. In her mind, the sightings were the only thing in her life that made sense.

*

Their singing woke her that night.

An unknown dialect. Not Gaelic. She'd been in Ireland long enough to pick up its inflections. The voices she heard were less lilting, with more consonants. Low and tantalising. Foreboding. Calling to her.

Tally sat up in her bed. Not bothering to change out of her pyjamas or put on shoes, she walked out of her hotel room into the lobby. It was busy with an overflow of noisy patrons from an adjoining pub. They didn't give Tally a second glance, accustomed to tourists and their eccentric ways.

Outside, she ponderously strode through moonlit streets, bare feet blackened by cobblestones and benumbed with cold, flesh stippled with goose pimples. She plodded on, following the voices until she reached the very edge of the Walk, where a series of steps led into the water. There she sat, the river licking at her toes.

They were waiting for her. A group swimming in circles, masses of Titian hair streaming over sloping shoulders, azure bellies soft where they merged into fishtails. The air smelled slightly of sulphur.

Tally wasn't frightened; rather, she was pervaded with a queer calmness, a sense of finality. One of the creatures swam over to Tally and outstretched its arms, small breasts rising. Leaning forward, Tally stared into the creature's dark sunken eyes. She stroked its wind-stung cheeks, kissed its lips and twined her fingers in its hair. The creature smiled. Tally heard herself laughing. The coldness in her feet spread to her shins and thighs, halting at her waist. Soothing, deadening coldness that blotted out all else, her loneliness and disquietude.

'Merrow,' Tally said, and dove into the water.

*

Her legs were discovered floating near the Walk the next morning. Cleanly detached from her body. A few days later, her pyjamas washed up on the shore of Mutton Island.

Of course, people conjectured that she'd been murdered. But the Gardaí maintained that her remains showed no signs of struggle or foul play. Hadn't her family back home said she was heartbroken? Wasn't she often seen at Galway's riverside, alone? Likely, she'd drowned and was eaten by fishes. Her torso was never found.

Time passed. The story faded from newspapers, eventually merging with folklore.

*

These days, travellers keep flocking to Galway's pubs and shops, the older-than-old stone buildings and outdoor marketplaces, the Spanish Arch and the Long Walk.

On occasion, people traversing the Walk see things in the River Corrib. Things they can't quite explain. Shimmers of red beneath the waves. Glistening blue skin, opalescent scales. And teeth spread in a smile.

WINTER SOLSTICE   ELIZABETH POWER

At the altar of man to worship man

There is a mass meaningless ritual
Stolen from us women
Next time you sit, submit
Know what you witness
Is older than you think

On a full moon on Máimin Mountain
Our breath carries our sounds
Our souls exhale and we remember

We remember, we remember
When churches were mountains
Solid cathedrals of life giving water
That came from stone high places of sacred
Repositories of soul
They stored the energy
They sheltered and circled the valley.

We remember, we remember
When mountains formed a chalice
Of menstrual blood at the moon's fullness.
In our high priestess power
Our song went from circle to circle
Mountain to mountain,
Valley to valley,
All over the country
We honoured the fullness of our cycle
We honoured the miracle

The transubstantiation
No priest would ever have
To bring life from our bodies
To bring life from our blood

MAGICAL THINKING   MELANIE POWER

That summer
was all long rides
and holy Ford silence,
the holy boredom of long
drives and the pines, the pines, the pines,
stark green stretches against the clean blue sky. That Ford

puttered its path to the west coast, the way
we knew not by heart but
by roadway sugar stops. My sister and I
played every game under the sun,
rebels against boredom, me learning
to love her syndrome. The houses are so
far apart in Three Rock Cove,
they all look   alone. My stepmom's home
is wood-fire warm, an empty nest since
she left. Her parents are fisherpeople here.
Awake before dawn, they brave the bay to comb the sea
for crab and cod through rain, drizzle, fog. On the way back
to town, the Ford mustered its last putts
of energy, old as me at thirteen and ready, too,
to retire from the loneliness of
long-distance drives. The car darkened as
we drove through tunnels and I awoke with
the Avalon light as a dozen birds
met the top of the Ford in staccato thuds.
Dad pulled over to floss their bodies
from the luggage racks. 'They are not dead,'
he said, 'they are sleeping.' About that
I choose to believe him.

GORILLA   FIONA PITT-KETHLEY

I soap him from head to toe, massage,
facial. He grunts like the animal he is.
This Western gorilla will never be clean.
I hide my Chinese name. He calls me May.

I come audibly when we are in bed.
The Madame orders this. He knows it's fake.
I know it's fake. It is the way.
I see him on top of me in the mirror.
There are mirrors everywhere. They line the walls.
Important clients like to see themselves.

I search his hair and half expect some nits.
Two condoms on his cock. I wish I could
cling film the rest. The thing I really fear's
a pubic hair stuck like a piece of floss
between my even pearly teeth.

BUTTERFLY
ANNE GRIFFIN

I knew something was up when I phoned and got no answer. Two days. That's how long I held off. Two days of convincing myself it was just your mobile on the blink, or you were out pottering in the garden, making the most of the fine weather. But the more I wished it, the more I knew my world, in which all I had to worry about was buying more Ready Brek on the way home from work, was slowly slipping away. Again.

After I read Jess her story that evening, for once letting her arms hug my neck for as long as she wanted, I rang Derek, your buddy next door. He kept me on the phone as he let himself in with the spare, confirming the worst. I cried in the downstairs loo, holding my hand to my mouth in case Keith heard me.

'Just popping round to Mam's, babes,' I called to him, when I eventually came out, with just enough in me to hold my voice steady. I ran before he had time to lower the volume on the TV. Let his calls go to voicemail. Wasn't ready, you see, to admit to myself, let alone him, we were back to square one.

When I got there you were lying on the couch. Face down. Head cocked to one side. Comatose. That manky dressing gown on you. In need of a good soak – like you. And the smell of the place. Alcohol, smoke and dog. Not that Riley was there. Derek said he'd take him. Reckoned he hadn't been fed or walked in a while. I opened the window behind you before reaching down to check there was still a pulse. There it was, your existence pumping away. Hunkering down, I lay my hand on your bird's nest hair from how many days of you not giving a monkey's as my eyes trailed the four empty Bulmers bottles lying on the floor.

-Mam? I said, so close that I could see that freckle on your neck. Dark, dark brown. I touched your cheek, your arm. Pushed a little harder but nothing.

-Mam, I said again, more a sigh than a prompt this time.

I left you a little while longer, making my way upstairs, half afraid of what I'd find, following the trail of empties: the landing, the loo, your bedroom windowsill, the heap of sick in the corner. I landed on your unmade bed. Sat there for a bit before slumping down sideways.

Your sheets still smelt of Chanel No. 5. Do you remember when I was little I'd get into the bed with you and Dad in the mornings? Up, Miss Sleepy, he'd say. Just one more minute, pleeeease. I'd be snuggled in tight, stroking the golden hairs of your arm. Just one, you'd say, just one. And then you'd wrap me up, so close I could smell your skin. Butterflies, I'd think, this is what beautiful butterflies smell like.

With my head on your pillow, I watched the soft, silent 'sorry to bother you' rain. The kind you hardly know is there only for the wet ground. I thought of the documentary about Thailand I'd seen the night before. Lotus flowers of the brightest, heart-stopping cerise that float on the lakes. Beautiful they were. I imagined those delicate drops falling onto the open flower like tiny diamonds catching in every dip and crevice. I closed my eyes and held their shimmer inside for as long as possible, shielding me from the growing knot in my stomach. When their force grew dim, I rose to the fate of you.

You came to after I'd straightened the place up a bit. Cleared the vomit, got rid of the bottles, washed up, opened every window. You shifted crankily in the gale and demanded to know what I was doing there.

-Derek called me, I lied. He was worried about you.

-Nosey fucker. You rubbed your nose with the back of your hand and looked about.

-Where's Riley? you asked, pissed off to find your dog missing.

-Derek has him. He's grand.

-Riley's mine. Not his.

You lay back, and cursed poor Derek a little more before blowing the hair out of your face. But it was having none of it and was back as quick, in the same place, over your nose and left cheek. I watched you pull an empty I'd missed from under you. Tilted it up toward the light, trying to see through the brown glass, squinting those beautiful brown eyes of yours that I've spent my life envying. You shook it one last hopeless time then flung it on the couch.

-I need more.

And there it was. The inevitable.

My eyes closed. And I breathed out through my nose. Not so heavy that you'd notice and start going off on one, but enough to buy me a bit of time.

-How 'bout I make you some tea? Yeah, that's what my deliberations had come up with: tea. Genius.

I got up to go in to the kitchen as quick as I could. Banged about with the mugs and the kettle and the tap and the fridge (waste of time) and the biscuit tin (like all you needed was a Jacob's Mikado). I came back to place your black tea on the coaster as far in from the edge of the coffee table as possible but still close enough to entice you. I looked at you, then it, and back again before pushing it an inch closer.

-Would ya leave the fucking tea? you said. The rage burned through you.

-It'll do you good, I tried.

You laughed. I took a sip of mine and watched you pick away at a thread from your dressing gown with your chipped nail. Your top lip curling up in pure disgust. Pick, pick. Pick, pick. Behind you on the bookshelf in a picture twenty-five years old the three of us smiled. You, me, Dad. Summer of '82. Courtown. You two with ninety-nines and me with a ball of pink candy floss bigger than my head.

You coughed and grunted on the coach. But I wouldn't heed you, unable to take my eyes from him. His blue soft tee shirt, some kind of cotton, I think we used to have sheets in the same material. I remember, touching it when he walked with his arm around me that holiday. I was stuck to him. Relishing the attention, feeling the little balls the fibre made and the heat and strength of his stomach. Loving it. Loving him. My six-foot-three undefeatable Dad. Except he was defeated, wasn't he? Two years ago, cancer. Ashes to ashes, dust to dust. You refused the very notion of a life without him. So you sold your soul to a bottle of Bacardi.

I squeezed my eyes against the sting of needing him, and missing you.

-I NEED fucking more, you said.

I could have said no. But I've done that how many times now. Calmly, angrily, lovingly, hatefully, every version, every relapse. Instead, I tried this:

-Ok. Where? Just like that, like it was the most natural thing to do, to feed this addict, this breaker of my heart.

-Aldi, you replied, your eyes narrowing, not trusting my surrender.

-You need to change, though.

You looked down at yourself, pushed one side of the gaping dressing gown in under the other and ran a hand through your hair.

-I'm grand.

-Jesus, Mam.

You blew me a kiss as you got up, too fast, too eager, and tripped over the leg of the table, the tea finding its inevitable fate on the carpet.

-Leave it, you demanded, as I hauled you up then rushed to the kitchen to get a cloth. You pulled me by the arm to the front door and out to my car without even stopping for your shoes.

The Aldi rose out of the darkness like a neon God. I imagined your liver clenching at the sight, begging for mercy. I pulled up to the double doors and out you stumbled, barefoot. You'd insisted you'd go in alone, not trusting me with your list. Here, here, leave me here, you said, pointing to the entrance. When I asked about money, you pulled your credit card from your bra and smiled.

After I parked, I went in anyway. Followed you around at a safe distance like a security guard. Head held high, you walked with determination, picking up a litre of Coke on the way. When you got to the beer, you took your twelve-pack of Galahad, placed a bottle of Old Hopking rum on its side on top, then the Coke in front, blocking it in. At the tills I stood well behind you, waiting for a fall or a bump, as nervous as when Jess started walking.

You got through, perfectly, ignoring the stares of the others in line and wishing the cashier 'A happy Christmas'. It was July. It wasn't until we were outside that it happened. The Coke, seeing its chance to escape, fell and frothed away down the tarmacked car park. I tried to get to you before you bent to retrieve it, but a shopper reversing a trolley out of its bay outside the exit hampered me. I saw you fall. A woman at the boot of her car put down her shopping and ran over. Finally released, I sprinted hard.

You were crying looking at the smashed bottle. Not caring that your knees were cut and your hands grazed, full of dirt and blood. You looked at me, so very devastated like Jess two days before when she'd dropped her ice cream. I bent my head to yours and rubbed your back. And as your forehead touched mine your hand rose to the top of my arm. You held on to it, squeezing it with whatever was left in you. And you sobbed. Big lonely, exhausted sobs.

-It's ok, Mam, I said, it's ok.

Eventually, I helped you up and brushed what dirt I could away. And as I retied your dressing gown, I found your eyes and smiled for them. I've got you now, they said, leave it to me. You sat in the passenger seat with the door open, pointing at the Galahad still upside down on the tarmac. I put the tray on your lap with the Coke. You tucked your arms around them, the most precious things in your world. Can we go now? you asked, looking up at me, defeated, lost. Sure, Mam, I said, patting your arm then closed the passenger door.

BEFORE ITS FIRST GRAVE THIS HILLSIDE
SIMON PERCHIK

Before its first grave this hillside
was already showing signs
let its slope escape as darkness

mistake every embrace for dirt
though one arm more than the other
is always heavier, still circles down

bringing you closer the way rain
knows winter will come with snow
that was here before, bring you weights

till nothing moves, not the shadows
not the sun coming here to learn
about the cold, hear the evenings.

GRATITUDE LINES   AUDREY MOLLOY

These breasts, crescent-moon minnow nets,
   low hills of a land once dreamt,
have emptied their full cream into fat babies,
   fleshy rivets for too many red mouths.
Yet free from scars, no tumours sown,
   responsive as switches, tasting of peaches.
Oh Calvin, La Perla, oh Agent Provocateur,
   how I love these breasts.

These silver filaments, too fine to call hairs,
   one for each night ended in a wicker chair,
the fine machinery of my middle ear ringing,
   lulled by a child's rapid breath and roast skin.
Yet here these children are, burning and breathing
   and see how they go on brightly burning!
Oh Clairol, oh Vidal, oh Moroccan Oil,
   how I love these hairs.

These legs, a daydreamer's assembly-line error,
   wrong size for my top half; too heavy of thigh,
beef to the heels like a Mullingar heifer,
   braided with veins of old maps or high cheese.
Yet so long and strong and how they have borne me
   and my piggy-backed young over daisy-spotted hills.
Oh Scarpa, oh Merrell, oh 60-Denier,
   how I love these legs.

These years, gorging like grubs on the fat of my cheeks,
   pleating their once petal-flesh into gratitude lines,
slowly pouring colour into progeny, until
   I'm no more than a clothes horse of old linen.

The milestone birthdays still come and go, counted
   in fives, now that we know there is no next safe level.
Oh Botox, La Prairie, oh Retinol A,
how I love the passing of these years.

MORPHOGENESIS   CATHERINE POWER-EVANS

t rolled between my feet. I held a gasp, watched as the thing rocked itself into stillness on the grass. Four minutes, I remembered, that's how long a body has before decomposition sets in after death. I'd Googled. Heart stops, oxygenation ceases. Carbon dioxide builds, kills cells. Enzymes flood the cells and they digest themselves. Amino acid soup.

The globe, with its polar indents sat bordered by a pair of red Converse parentheses, was a visual beginning and end. In the middle, a statement glaring rude and ruddy, punctuated with yellow pinpricks. Not dead yet, one minute left. Tick, tock. The last apple on the tree, its tenuous connection to life had perished and succumbed to one of Newton's laws. I knew he'd gone.

The planet ceased to rotate, stagnant in this thrumming human moment. Every hue, every buttermilk speckle of that apple's surface I scrutinised, mapped and stored while I bent to gather breath. I wondered which tissue, which exact molecule relinquished its grip. Alone, that fruit remained while its cohorts departed thud by dull thud on the brown-tinged lawn. An upbeat startle broke an unnatural cocoon of inertia. Pharrell might have been 'Happy', but I had no inclination to sing.

'Hello?' I answered. My sister's name was bright light capitals. While I waited, expectant and dread-filled, a cacophony of sirens blared from my upturned palm. At the hospital, still. I didn't go in the ambulance. Couldn't. Though there was no reason for her to verbalise the news, I heard her ragged voice confirm what my bones knew. I nodded. Wordless, I hung up and stared at the screen until the liquid crystals darkened.

On a couple of gnarled limbs dripping over the stream, robins chirped to each other. A male and female, a devoted brace. Today, their song rang cheerless to my ear. The chill crept beneath the fleeced edges of my hoody, wetting the skin of my neck and chest that had, until then, been protected. Salt-gunked, my face stung and though I tried hard, I couldn't make it better.

When I stopped rubbing the tears tingling on freckles, I noticed the stark, denuded branches appear shocked at the screaming absence of apples. Mosaic thoughts shape-shifted, morphed while I studied papery oak leaves weep onto the shed. They settled, the new burying the old, layer upon layer of mulch fodder. A long, low sound emanated from deep inside and I buckled under a tsunami of sorrow cascading through my whole being. Legs which my mother maintained I'd 'robbed off a giraffe' collapsed at their denim-clad hinges and crashed me to the ground. The smell of dampness and mush filtered up to my nostrils.

'I'll try and hold on till autumn's finished, pet. Another push is all I need, I'll have a talk with meself so I don't miss your twenty-first birthday.' Determination ploughed his bronzed features as he made me his promise, and the utter nobility of his efforts killed me. It wasn't meant to be like that; I had everything on the iPad. All his appointments, meds; the notes all taken from each consultation. He'd laugh at me when the notification came up for his medication, or for him to do physiotherapy exercises. Lists written down on a diary and ticked off through the day, with keen attention to blood sugars and the timing of meals.

'What does that noisy thing say I have to do now?' he'd ask. Everything I could do, I did. Nothing could go wrong, I had reduced all the risks. Except it did go wrong; a simple thing like missing the toilet and slipping on the wet floor had devastating results on a fragile skull.

'Sur, it's hard to kill a bad thing!' Although he laughed, I couldn't muster more than a faint smile. If only I hadn't left him shuffle to the loo on his own, if only I'd ... Yesterday, when I gave him birthday cake it was autumn. Today, I saw the last of the leaf months fall off my virtual calendar.

'Winter,' I whispered. That hateful phase of stinking, pernicious putrefaction and overwhelming withering. At the final season of his existence grey, ravaging winter came in search of my grandfather. It claimed his last cell.

THE THEFT   CHARLES WILKINSON

– reports of yourself seen strolling in a foreign city
or captured on grainy grey film: a lean figure, hat
drawn down if leaving a bank & head bowed.
Caught on nothing more than cameras, he travels
with your name on his passport. That statement
before the card was stopped tells of a taste for
Italian cuisine, tickets for the theatre, baroque
hotels & casinos.

       At dawn, draining the account,
he stole wealth & then your story; those names
given and inherited, the first gifts, saving life;
a part of the self is now cancelled along with
the credit. Such facility he shows, consuming
the years on another's behalf. He knows towns,
cities, airports in every continent. The cuckoo,
constructed in the nest of numbers & hatched
in silence,
         flies in your missing feathers.
      In the night, dream of a double:
        your face, foul-bending above,
          with a Judas kiss.

WELCOME   FRED JOHNSTON

i.m. Judee Sill

Now is the toll-booth
with its basket for spare change
yellow barrier like a border crossing
and beyond, the last run home

Now the foot pressing out
a glad acceleration
eyed by neon watchtowers –
the night territories avoided, passed
far small lights over black fields
mark where jaded others undress
TVs turn themselves off
'phones perish unanswered

Now too the tunnel
entered like a rape –
under the river's skirts
a fingering of headlights, groan of gears
After this, the crass familiarity
of sniffling rubber on a bed of gravel:
all day we've waited for this

Now the house so predictably dead,
rain prostitutes itself
in the drains, the smell of sex
rising out of the wet gardens
the engine cooling, calming
out of breath. I'm home. Welcome me.

MARION'S EDGE   LES WICKS

No one touched her, it seemed
a consensus that her pain's weight would
infect & weaken
all our certainties.

She wanted it,
our consolation.
There had been a journey
until she fell off.

At the basement concert
her music was too strong
for those timid pastel walls.
We all flaked.

When she & I shared a smoke together
it was the words that smouldered
on a Persian carpet
inscribed with flammable verses.

Marion once tried dancing
at the *Strip Palace* but the punters
looked away while the spotlight-guy's hands
shook glare all over the ceiling.

Barely 21, her job had become trips
to hospital, endless bloodwork.
Pieces of her were shuffled away
on crisp plastic trays.

autumn 2017

We never asked.
Perhaps jealous of her extremity.
Knew her door
was already opening.

Turns out nothing costs nothing.

ENCOUNTER AT DHARAVI SLUM KATHY ROBERTSON

My seven-week vacation throughout the Indian subcontinent is coming to an end. I've become seasoned to the daily assault of cows, manure, tuk tuks, and rickshaws. I've visited spice markets, museums, temples. Rode a camel in Rajasthan, past golden mustard crops, to attend a village wedding. Toured majestic Taj Mahal inlaid with jewels. Joined an elephant procession up the sloping entrance to Amber Fort in Jaipur. Sailed Mother Ganges past the crematorium of Varanasi. Sat in awe of the Dalai Lama in Dharamsala surrounded by red-robed monks. It's been exhilarating. Uplifting. Shocking. All at the same time.

I've saved a trip to Dharavi Slum for last. I'm reluctant, yet compelled. Question my motives for going to such a place. How can I intrude on others' distress? Ogle at their misfortune? After all, it isn't like I'm going as a benefactress bearing gifts of goodwill. Yet I *do* want to take a look. Gain insight into what poverty really looks like. At least that's what I tell myself. And so, taking a deep breath, I join the tour to this abject site just beyond the glittering lights of Mumbai.

As we head out, my mind reflects on these past weeks in India. One thing I won't forget is the incessant honking of car horns. It's deafening. Stickers proclaim HORN PLEASE on the back of cars. And the masses are glad to oblige. This persistent cacophony can fray the hardiest of nerves. With a population of over a billion people, there is a crushing array on the move. Bombarded with relentless barking, twenty-four seven.

Without question, meeting the people across this vast land has been the highlight. I admire the women. Their shy smiles. Giggles behind silk veils. Gossip in friendly groups. Children close at hand. Some toil in rice fields without complaint. Balance wood and bricks on their head. Charcoal hair braided into soft coil. Others welcome me into their elegant homes. Offer finest delicacies. Introduce me to extended family. Such pride. And those haunting eyes, chocolate windows to the soul.

I've observed the men as they gather at the local mosque for prayer. Sell their wares at open marketplaces. Smoke bongs in shops. Bribe sellers for various acquisitions. Drink chai tea. Play cricket. Their kinship is most striking. A solid fraternity. Camaraderie of old and young interacting with affectionate banter. Often holding hands. Arm in arm. A sense they've got each other's back.

Yet it's the children who've captured my heart. They're attracted to me like babes to breast. Everywhere I go. They surround me with playful abandon. Laugh. Want to take my picture. They dream of a singular profession, whether boy or girl, *Doctor!* They're warm-hearted. Genuine. I'm touched by their generosity of spirit. In truth, I adore them all.

Now the underbelly of India awaits. The guide barks orders as we approach Dharavi Slum. *Remain inside locked van. Leave windows up. Don't converse with beggars.* I begin to wonder if being swarmed by the poor, children as well as adults, is bad for business. Too sensitive for western mores.

I can't look away. The squalor is horrific, yet mesmerising. As I stare out of the van, I try to comprehend the depth of privation that stretches before me. The clamour of masses living in this putrid place is incomprehensible to the eye, one million within each square mile. Makeshift shacks, by the hundreds of thousands, stretch into the horizon. They stand like decks of stacked cards, ready to topple over. A mixture of mud and cow dung cover their walls and floors. Families sleep side by side, wall to wall. Ruptured pipes ooze slimy water into the streets. Barefoot children play atop dumpsters. Stray animals, cows, goats, dogs, defecate at random. Dwellers use rivers and alleyways as lavatories since there is only one toilet for a thousand people. Laundry dangles from lines outside stoops, faded and worn. Dharavi swarms with the bile of humanity. Hot, dirty, smelly.

I marvel that Dharavi exists right in the shadow of Mumbai, formerly Bombay, a financial centre and India's largest city. Originally the land was a mangrove swamp inhabited by Koli fishermen. Over time rotten fish, coconut leaves and human waste clogged the marsh until the Kolis had to abandon their livelihood. Soon other migrants moved in. Since slum dwellers don't have legal status, they're not entitled to public services. Forced to deal with racketeers for water and electricity.

As I gape, stupefied by the gaggle of deprivation before me, a woman's face appears at my window pressing face to pane. Voyeur to voyeur. I recoil as if struck by a cobra. The toothless beggar is probably around my age but appears much older. Destitute. Her emaciated body wrapped in rags. Caked skin. Matted hair.

Her gaze penetrates my soul. I shift uneasily as she gapes at me sitting in air-conditioned comfort during the height of India's oppressive heat. Plush seats. Cool drink in hand. I become self-conscious of my travel clothes, breathable material with sun ray protection. In fact, workers had collected my laundry outside my Mumbai guest house door during the night and returned it, pressed and folded, just that morning. Clothes scrubbed to perfection at Dhobi Ghat, the world's largest outdoor laundry.

Fate has dictated this vagrant's cruel existence. She's a Dalit. Lowest rung on the Untouchable caste system. Condemned to do the grimiest jobs, scrub latrines, strip animal carcasses. Like her forebears. A centuries-old practice. She lives in fear lest her shadow even cross the path of a higher caste member. Forbidden. Disturbs the karma of others.

I ponder the woman's childhood. Was she a street-smart urchin, wise to the pangs of starvation? Sent off as a child to beg so her family could nibble on a stale crust of bread? Does she have children of her own, begging on the streets as she is doing now? I admire her resilience in the face of so much suffering.

We are two women partitioned by glass. One a victim of her birth. The other a beneficiary of privilege. My shame is palpable.

The beggar balls her fingers together and moves her hand towards her mouth. I am intuitively aware of her request. *Food!*

The driver glances in his rear-view mirror just as I reach into my purse. Before I can protest, he plunges his foot on the gas pedal. The van catapults into the distance, leaving a grimy tornado in its wake. Rupees land in a heap on the van's floor.

THE CRANNÓG QUESTIONNAIRE MARY O'DONNELL

How would you introduce yourself as a writer to those who may not know you?

It always depends on the person who doesn't know me. I've become better at simply introducing myself as a full-time author if the question arises. I mention 'full-time' because that fends off any doubts the person has about what kind of writer you are. A small number of people are surprised to discover that I've published whatever number of books, despite just having heard me describe myself as a full-time author, so sometimes I do wonder where the credibility gap is and if they think some writers write to pass the time!!

When did you start writing?

I always wrote even as a child, then as a teenager. There was good validation to the activity of writing in our house.

Do you have a writing routine?

I write in the mornings from 10 – 1.30. After that anything else I produce after a raid on the fridge, followed by a half hour rest on the couch, is really tweaking words, or perhaps preparing a few lines to remind myself, in the case of fiction, what I might do the following morning. Then I try to just stop working and free my mind a little.

When you write, do you picture somehow a potential audience or do you just write?

I just write. I know anyway that it's mostly women who read my fiction (mostly but not exclusively) but I don't think about that either. I haven't a clue who reads my poetry. Again, I don't consider potential audiences because if I did it would inhibit me. The act of writing for me is a compulsion that makes me feel connected to something unnameable. It is necessary, and audience considerations are beyond me while I'm in the middle of something.

Some writers describe themselves as planners, while others plunge right in to the writing. Would you consider yourself a planner or a plunger?

I'm a plunger, who may have collected small scraps of random information without realising beforehand that they were going to be relevant to what I'm about to write! The random bits could be newspaper cuttings, phrases, new words, actual objects, links to music, and have been fossils and pieces of quartz in the case of one novel that evolved (The Elysium Testament, 1999, Trident Press). I rarely have a novel entirely planned out, and I never know how it will end either.

How important are names to you in your books? Do you choose the names based on liking the way they sound or for the meaning? Do you have any name-choosing resources you recommend?

The names of my characters do matter to me. I am aware of my own aversion to certain names, especially fashionable ones, so I have to distance myself from that. And names can be socially significant, of course. So, if you have a male character and call him 'Sledge' or 'Moro' that tells the reader something about class (perhaps). Call him 'Matthew' or 'Donal' and that presents a different impression. With women, a 'Tracey' or 'Chardonnay' (à la Katie Hopkins!) suggests quite a different type from an 'Eithne', a 'Medhbh', or a 'Rose'.

Is there a certain type of scene that's harder for you to write than others? Love? Action? Erotic?

I believe I have a gift for crowd scenes in which something important is revealed, and in three of my four novels this has been the case. I discovered this capacity as a short-story writer, long ago, and realised that I quite enjoyed keeping my eye on the ball while dealing with crowds, groups, or several characters in particular scenes.

Tell us a bit about your non-literary work experience please.

I have some non-literary work experience, as a teacher of German and English at second level in the 1980s, as a personal assistant to various people during the early 80s recession, and as a library assistant at the then NUI

Maynooth. I also worked in Concern's head office for a time. But gradually most of my work was connected to literary life. I presented various poetry programmes for RTÉ Radio, which, obviously, I scripted. I worked as the Sunday Tribune's Drama Critic, then in freelance journalism, and then more and more began to teach Creative Writing – most recently on Galway University's MA in Creative Writing.

What do you like to read in your free time?
Both fiction and non-fiction. I read little new poetry and concentrate mostly on poetry that actually pleases me. I like experimental poetry that is clearly trying to, well, 'experiment', which is what we should all do as poets. Regarding fiction, I don't often read the latest raved-about novels and short story collections unless I have a personal connection with the author. Often I prefer to wait until I'm ready and uninfected by hype.

What one book do you wish you had written?
The Great Gatsby.

Do you see writing short stories as practice for writing novels?
No, not in the least, though I know that in my own case I did write short stories before I wrote a novel. But a short story is as different or as similar to a novel as a poem is as different or as similar to a short story, if you get my drift. Poem and short story share certain concerns, among them brevity and concision, space for the lyrical and also for narrative. But the scale of the novel, although it shares narrative concerns with the short story, has to scale very different levels of credibility. These are achieved through the handling of time, for one thing, and through large-scale events (not literally events, but episodes and turning points) that simply could not be incorporated into shorter fiction. And although character can indeed be thoroughly explored in short fiction, there is more space for many characters of depth within a novel.

Do you think writers have a social role to play in society or is their role solely artistic?
I think we are a little like unofficial liars. We take ourselves away from the group (or tribe, if we look on it as an anthropological phenomenon and think

103

of storytellers) and go off into a corner (meaning artists' retreat, your study, or a cave in the back of beyond) and weave these yarns which we hope our group will be drawn to and from which they might discover new ways for themselves to see and dream. Objectively speaking, it may be a semi-social role, but one isn't conscious of it during the act of writing.

Tell us something about your latest publication, please.

In July, 451 Editions reissued my 1992 debut novel, The Light Makers. I really just wanted to get this book back in print, twenty-five years later, as I felt it might well be enjoyed by a new generation of readers. Its themes are certainly relevant and it has a strong undercurrent of feminism which carries my protagonist Hanna Troy right to the end. I'm delighted by this novel, which I hadn't read for years. It was like revisiting a younger self and discovering how she wrote, years after you'd forgotten. The cover is fabulous, by the way, and it's available in some bookshops and online and for Kindle.

Can writing be taught?

Writing can be taught to someone who is hungry to write and who possesses some talent. Not all published writers are talented, remember. Some are, some are less so. But hunger and an appetite for reading and expression in language will carry the right person a long way. What talent is, is sometimes elusive, but those who have it really do rise.

Have you given or attended creative writing workshops? If you have, share your experiences a bit please.

The first two workshops I attended as an apprentice writer were interesting in different ways. Julia O'Faolain ran the first one. She was a good teacher and you knew you were in the presence of someone with an excellent mind and a certain rigour of approach. The second one was a poetry workshop and I came away from it on a high, because the teacher gave such encouragement. There were others, one in which I observed the teacher diminish a woman (the administrator), for no obvious reason other than pettishness, I felt. It's always interesting to see how much clay our heroes and heroines in literature have between their toes!

As a writing teacher I've led groups everywhere, in Ireland, and abroad.

Participants have changed since I taught writing for the first time in 1983. And over the years I've watched how participants expect more and come with a more usefully critical literary vocabulary than heretofore. Often they are working people, not unemployed, and often they are very directed and focused too. In the past, American students were easier to work with because they understood the language of critical discourse, but Irish participants and students are very tuned-in nowadays, and have other cultural, native advantages at their disposal.

Flash fiction – how driven is the popularity of this form by social media like Twitter and its word limits? Do you see Twitter as somehow leading to shorter fiction?
I don't read a lot of flash fiction, although I've read some pieces I thought were so perfect, among them work from Nuala O'Connor. I don't think Twitter is the link to shorter fiction, so much as paucity of time.

Finally, what question do you wish that someone would ask about your writing, and how would you answer it?
I'd like them to ask, 'Well, Mary, and how has it been for you?'

Finally, finally, some Quick Pick Questions:

> **E-books or print?** *Both*
> **Dog or cat?** *Both*
> **Reviews – read or don't read?** *Read some*
> **Best city to inspire a writer?** *Paris*
> **Favourite meal out: breakfast, lunch, dinner?** *Lunch (long!)*
> **Weekly series or box sets?** *Box sets*
> **Favourite colour?** *Vermilion*
> **Rolling Stones or Beatles?** *Beatles*
> **Night or day?** *Night with the hope of day*

Artist's Statement

Cover image: *Resistance* by Jayashree Rai

Jayashree Rai, a native of India, is an artist and art instructor. She lived in England, Germany and Saudi Arabia before moving to Canada in 2007. She works in all mediums and enjoys experimenting with many different techniques. However, she has a special love of watercolour, and through her subtle and free-flowing style, she is able to capture the mood of her subjects. She has received many commendations for her art and in 1992 one of her artworks, *The Falconer*, was selected as a UNICEF greeting card.

Biographical Details

Justin Allen was born in Bakersfield, California in 1979. He earned a BA in English at San Francisco State University, and has worked as an editor, designer, and technologist for leading arts, activist, and news organisations. He co-founded the online travel and culture magazine *The Creosote Journal* in 2011 and currently runs a creative technology blog called Forwardslash. His writing has appeared in *Fiddleblack*, *Transfer*, the *Sacramento News & Review*, the *San Francisco Public Press*, and other publications.

Amanda Bell's début poetry collection, *First the Feathers*, will be published by Doire Press in November 2017. Her haibun collection *Undercurrents* (Alba, 2016) won second prize in the HSA Merit Book Awards and was shortlisted for a Touchstone Distinguished Books Award. Her children's book, *The Lost Library Book*, was published by The Onslaught Press, 2017.

Patrick Chapman is the author of seven poetry collections and three books of fiction. His latest publications are *Slow Clocks of Decay* (Salmon Poetry, 2016), a radio adventure *Dan Dare: Operation Saturn* (B7 Productions, London, 2017), and a novel, *So Long, Napoleon Solo* (BlazeVOX Books, NY, 2017).

Trevor Conway writes mainly poems, stories and songs. He posts to his website/blog, trevorconway.weebly.com, occasionally. His first collection of poems, *Evidence of Freewheeling*, was published by Salmon Poetry in 2015.

Colin Dardis is a poet, editor and freelance arts facilitator from Northern Ireland. He co-runs Poetry NI, and is editor for *Lagan Online*. One of Eyewear Publishing's Best New British and Irish Poets 2016, a collection with Eyewear, *the x of y*, is forthcoming in 2018.

Laura Del Col Brown is originally from West Virginia in the United States, but now lives in London. Her work has previously appeared in publications including the *DSCH Journal*, *Poor Yorick Journal* and *Maudlin House*, and six of her poems have been included in the UK-based Poem Flyer project. When not writing, she works for a bat conservation charity.

Catherine Edmunds' published works include a poetry collection, four novels and a Holocaust memoir. She has twice been nominated for a Pushcart Prize, three times shortlisted in the Bridport, and has been published in many journals, including *The Frogmore Papers*, *Aesthetica*, *The Binnacle*, *Butchers' Dog*, and *Ambit*.

Kate Ennals is a poet and short-story writer and has both published in a range of journals including *Crannóg*, *Skylight 47*, *The Honest Ulsterman*, *Anomaly*, *Burning Bush 2*, *Poets Meet Politics*, *The International Lakeview Journal*, *Boyne Berries*, *North West Words*, etc. Her first collection of poetry *At The Edge* was published in 2015. She has lived in Ireland for 25 years and currently runs poetry and writing workshops in County Cavan, and organises At The Edge, Cavan, a literary reading evening, funded by the Cavan Arts Office.

Rebecca Gethin has published two pamphlets in 2017: *All the Time in the World* (Cinnamon Press) and *A Sprig of Rowan* (Three Drops Press). She has previously published two other collections and two novels. She was awarded a Hawthornden Scholarship in 2016 and runs the Poetry School's monthly seminars in Plymouth, UK.

Anne Griffin's work has appeared in *The Irish Times*, *The Stinging Fly*, *For Books' Sake*, *The Weekend Read*, and *The Lonely Crowd* amongst others. She was shortlisted for the Hennessy New Irish Writing Award and The Sunday Business Post Short Story

Competition. Her long-lists include The Fish Publishing Short Story Award and The Seán Ó Faoláin Short Story Competition. She is a recent graduate of the MA in Creative Writing Programme in UCD.

Patrick Hansel has published poems, stories and essays in over 40 journals and anthologies, including *The Meadowland Review, The Transnational, Isthmus, Red Weather Review, Ash & Bones* and *Lunch Ticket*. He has received awards from the Loft Literary Center in Minneapolis and the MN State Arts Board, and his novella *Searching* was serialised in 33 issues of *The Alley News*. He is the editor of *The Phoenix of Phillips* literary magazine, a new journal for and by the people of the most diverse neighbourhood in Minneapolis.

Maureen Hill is a retired teacher living in Belfast. Her work has been published in several anthologies and in magazines, including *The Stinging Fly, Orbis, South, The French Literary Review*, and *Abridged*.

Ann Howells has edited *Illya's Honey* for eighteen years, recently taking it digital: www.IllyasHoney.com. Her publications are: *Black Crow in Flight* (Main Street Rag), *Under a Lone Star* (Village Books), *Letters for My Daughter* (Flutter), and *Cattlemen & Cadillacs* (Dallas Poets Community), an anthology of D/FW poets she edited. Her chapbook manuscript, *Softly Beating Wings*, won the William D. Barney Memorial Chapbook Contest 2017 and was released in June.

Ellen Kelly is a sociologist, writer and blogger. Her competition-winning short stories have been published by Creative Writing Ink online, by Original Writing.ie in an anthology, and by *The Irish Times* as part of Hennessy New Irish Writing. She is shortlisted for a Hennessy Award in the category of Emerging Writers in 2018. Another story was broadcast on RTÉ Radio 1 as part of the Francis MacManus Short Story Competition. She lives in Dublin. She is represented by literary agent Ivan Mulcahy of Mulcahy Associates, London.

Shannon Kelly's work has appeared in *Crannóg, The Irish Times*, and *BODY*, Prague. She was the 2016 winner of the Allingham Festival Poetry Competition. Originally from the USA, she lives in Galway, Ireland.

Aoibheann McCann has published short fiction in several national and international literary magazines including *Crannóg*. She has had stories included in the anthologies *No Love Lost* and *The Body I Live In*, published by Pankhurst Press, UK. Her story *Johnny Claire* was shortlisted for the WOW! Awards, 2015.

Neil McCarthy is a poet from west Cork, who, having served his time in Galway, now lives in Vienna. His poems have appeared in numerous journals across the world and his debut collection *Stopgap Grace* is due out in spring 2018. www.neilmccarthypoetry.com

Michael McGlade has been published in *The Saturday Evening Post, Confrontation, Hennessy New Irish Writing*, and *Grain*. He holds a master's degree in English and Creative Writing from the Seamus Heaney Centre, Queen's University, Belfast. He is represented by the Blake Friedmann Literary Agency and is a Professional member of the Irish Writers Centre.

Tim Miller's most recent poetry has appeared in *Londongrip, The High Window, Poethead, Cumberland River Review, The Basil O'Flaherty, Albatross, The Journal* (Wales), and others. The complete collection of his poems from old Europe, *Bone, Antler, Stone*, will be published in 2018 by The High Window Press. He writes about religion, history and poetry at www.wordandsilence.com.

Audrey Molloy was born in Dublin and grew up in Blackwater, County Wexford. She now lives in Sydney, where she works as a medical writer and editor. Her poetry has recently appeared in *Australian Poetry Anthology, The Galway Review, Ink, Sweat & Tears* and *Orbis*. She was shortlisted for the 2016 Judith Wright Poetry Prize for New and Emerging Poets and for the 2016 Over the Edge New Writer of the Year.

Suri Parmar is a Toronto-based writer and filmmaker. She is an alumna of the Canadian Film Centre and the Stonecoast MFA Program in Creative Writing. Her short films have screened at film festivals around the world.

Simon Perchik is an attorney whose poems have appeared in *Partisan Review, Forge, Poetry, Osiris, The New Yorker* and elsewhere. His most recent collection is *The Osiris Poems* published by box of chalk, 2017. For more information, including free e-books, his essay titled *Magic, Illusion and Other Realities* please visit his website at www.simonperchik.com.

Fiona Pitt-Kethley is the author of more than 20 books of prose or poetry and has written for many of the best UK papers. Her poem is part of a proposed collection, *Around the World in Eighty Lays*. She lives in Spain.

Elizabeth Power is a graduate of MA in Writing (2007) from National University of Ireland, Galway. She has won or been placed in fiction competitions including Swift Satire International Writing Competition, Dromineer International Literary Festival and Maria Edgeworth Literary Competition. She has been published widely in national Irish literary journals including *The Moth, Crannóg* and in the anthology *Noir by Noir West* (Arlen House). Her poetry has appeared in *Skylight 47, Force Ten, Three Drops from a Cauldron* (UK), and *Shelia-Na-Gig* (US).

Melanie Power is a poet from St John's, Newfoundland. Her poetry has been featured in *Southward Journal, Headlight Anthology, Soliloquies Anthology*, and *(parenthetical)*, as well as forthcoming elsewhere. She writes from Montréal, Québec, where she is pursuing an MA in English Literature, specialising in poetry, at Concordia University.

Catherine Power Evans writes short stories and poetry. Her work appears in print and online in *Silver Apples, The Linnet's Wings* and elsewhere. She was longlisted for the 2017 Colm Tóibín Short Story Award.

John Reinhart is a Frequent Contributor at the Songs of Eretz Poetry Review and recipient of the 2016 Horror Writers Association Dark Poetry Scholarship. His work has been nominated for multiple Rhysling and Dwarf Stars Awards. To date, he has penned four collections of poetry, most recently *broken bottle of time* (Alban Lake, 2017). Find his work at http://home.hampshire.edu/~jcr00/reinhart.html and @JReinhartPoet

Karen Rigby is the author of *Chinoiserie* (Ahsahta Press). Her poems have appeared in *The London Magazine, Field, jubilat* and other journals. Born in the Republic of Panama, she now lives in Arizona. www.karenrigby.com

Kathy Robertson is an award-winning writer whose works have appeared in literary journals, anthologies, newspapers, and magazines. She is a member of The Ontario Poetry Society, Tower Poetry Society, and the Cambridge Writers' Collective. Her B.Ed. is from the University of Western Ontario. She attained her BA at Wilfrid Laurier University, Waterloo, Ontario where she graduated with an English major and a double minor in history/psychology.

Robyn Rowland's poetry appears in national and international journals including *Poetry Ireland Review* and *THE SHOp* and in over forty anthologies, including eight editions of *Best Australian Poems*. Her latest books are *Line of Drift*, Doire Press, 2015, and her bi-lingual *This Intimate War Gallipoli/Çanakkale 1915 – İçli Dışlı Bir Savaş: Gelibolu/Çanakkale 1915* published by Five Islands Press in Australia and by Bilge Kultur Sanat in Turkey, sponsored by the Municipality of Çanakkale. Turkish translation is by Mehmet Ali Çelikel. She has read in many countries including Bosnia, Serbia, Austria, Turkey, Canada, India, and Portugal. Her work is on film at the National Irish Poetry Archives, James Joyce Library, UCD.

Benjamin Smith grew up in Hebden Bridge, UK. He currently lives in Bogota, Colombia. His work has previously appeared, or is forthcoming, in *The Meadow, Rust+Moth, Gravel, Menacing Hedge, Vayavya*, and elsewhere.

Bobbie Sparrow was longlisted for the Over the Edge new writers award in 2015 and 2016 and shortlisted for the Galway University Hospital Poetry Competition 2016. Her poems have been published in *Orbis, Picaroon, Skylight 47* and *The Rose Magazine*. She is a member of the online poetry group, Poets Abroad.

Michael Spring is the author of four poetry books. His third book, *Root of Lightning*, was awarded an honourable mention for the 2012 Eric Hoffer Book Award. His fourth book, *Unfolding the Field*, was published in 2016. He's won numerous awards, including the Robert Graves Award, the Turtle Island Poetry Award, and a Luso-American Fellowship from DISQUIET International. His poems have appeared in *Atlanta Review, Flyway, Gargoyle, Iota, Spillway*, and others. He lives in Oregon where he is a natural builder and a martial art instructor. He is also a poetry editor for the *Pedestal Magazine* and the Editor-in-chief for Flowstone Press.

Peter Stuart-Sheppard was nominated for a 2015 Forward Prize for poetry, and was highly commended in the 2016 Gregory O'Donoghue International Poetry Competition. His poetry has appeared in journals in Canada and Ireland including *The Literary Review of Canada, The Stinging Fly, Contemporary Verse 2, The Antigonish Review, Southword Journal* and previously in *Crannóg*. He lives in Toronto.

Ojo Taiye was born and grew up in Kaduna. He currently lives in Agbor, Delta State. He is a poet, essayist and teaches Tourism in Calvary Group of Schools, Agbor. His poems and works have appeared in journals like *Kalahari Review, Brittle Paper, Glass Journal, Tuck Magazine, Lunaris Review, Elsewhere, Eunoia Review, Lit Mag, Juke, Praxis Magazine* and elsewhere.

Laura Treacy Bentley is a poet, novelist, and a point-and-shoot photographer. Born in Hagerstown, Maryland, she was raised in Huntington, West Virginia, and graduated from Marshall University. Laura divides her time between the mountains of West Virginia and a log cabin in western Maryland. She is the author of a poetry collection, *Lake Effect*, a psychological thriller set in Ireland, *The Silver Tattoo*, a short-story prequel to her novel,

Night Terrors, and an art book of her poems and photographs, *Looking for Ireland: An Irish-Appalachian Pilgrimage, 2017*. lauratreacybentley.com.

Christine Valters Paintner's poems have been published in *The Galway Review, Boyne Berries, Headstuff, Skylight 47, Spiritus Journal, Tiferet, Anchor, Presence*. She was shortlisted for the Over the Edge New Writer of the Year twice and came second in the Galway University Hospital Arts Trust competition. AbbeyoftheArts.com.

Steve Wade's fiction has been published in over forty print publications including *The Irish Times, The Sunday Tribune, The Westmeath Examiner, Crannóg, Boyne Berries, Zenfri Publications, New Fables, Gem Street, Grey Sparrow, Fjords Arts and Literary Review*, and *Aesthetica Creative Works Annual*, 2011 and 2015. He was a prize nominee for the PEN/O. Henry Award, 2011, and a prize nominee for the Pushcart Prize, 2013. www.stephenwade.ie

Bogusia Wardein is from Poland. Her poems have been published in *The Rialto, Stand, Poetry Wales, THE SHOp* and other journals, as well as anthologies including *Hallelujah for 50ft Women*, Bloodaxe, 2015. Her website is www.bogusiawardein.com.

Les Wicks has performed at festivals, schools, prison etc. for over 40 years. His work has been published in over 350 magazines, anthologies & newspapers across 28 countries in 13 languages. He conducts workshops and runs Meuse Press which focuses on poetry outreach projects like poetry on buses and poetry published on the surface of a river. His 13th book of poetry is *Getting By Not Fitting In* (Island, 2016). leswicks@hotmail.com. http://leswicks.tripod.com/lw.htm

Charles Wilkinson's work includes *The Pain Tree and Other Stories* (London Magazine Editions). His poems have appeared in *Poetry Wales, Poetry Salzburg, The SHOp, Crannóg, Gargoyle, The Raintown Review, The Reader* and other journals. A pamphlet, *Ag & Au*, came out from Flarestack Poets. He lives in Powys, Wales. charliewilk@outlook.com

Kristin Camitta Zimet is the author of *Take in My Arms the Dark* and the editor of *The Sow's Ear Poetry Review*. Her poems are in journals including *Poet Lore, Salamander*, and *Natural Bridge*. She is also a reiki healer, visual artist, and master naturalist.

Stay in touch with

Crannóg

www.crannogmagazine.com

Lightning Source UK Ltd.
Milton Keynes UK
UKOW04f1801250917
309848UK00001B/52/P